The Story of the Odyssey

Alfred John Church and Homer

Alpha Editions

This edition published in 2024

ISBN : 9789362993489

Design and Setting By
Alpha Editions
www.alphaedis.com
Email - info@alphaedis.com

As per information held with us this book is in Public Domain.
This book is a reproduction of an important historical work. Alpha Editions uses the best technology to reproduce historical work in the same manner it was first published to preserve its original nature. Any marks or number seen are left intentionally to preserve its true form.

Contents

INTRODUCTION ....- 1 -

CHAPTER I THE COUNSEL OF ATHENE ....- 3 -

CHAPTER II THE ASSEMBLY ....- 7 -

CHAPTER III NESTOR ....- 11 -

CHAPTER IV IN SPARTA ....- 14 -

CHAPTER V MENELAUS'S TALE ....- 17 -

CHAPTER VI ULYSSES ON HIS RAFT ....- 21 -

CHAPTER VII NAUSICAA ....- 27 -

CHAPTER VIII ALCINOUS ....- 30 -

CHAPTER IX THE PHAEACIANS ....- 33 -

CHAPTER X THE CYCLOPS ....- 38 -

CHAPTER XI AEOLUS; THE LAESTRYGONS; CIRCE ....- 45 -

CHAPTER XII THE DWELLINGS OF THE DEAD ....- 51 -

CHAPTER XIII THE SIRENS; SCYLLA; THE OXEN OF THE SUN ....- 54 -

CHAPTER XIV ITHACA ....- 60 -

CHAPTER XV EUMAEUS, THE SWINEHERD .... - 66 -

CHAPTER XVI THE RETURN OF TELEMACHUS ....- 71 -

CHAPTER XVII ULYSSES AND TELEMACHUS ....- 74 -

CHAPTER XVIII ULYSSES IN HIS HOME ....- 79 -

CHAPTER XIX ULYSSES IN HIS HOME ....- 83 -

CHAPTER XX ULYSSES IS DISCOVERED BY HIS NURSE ....- 85 -

CHAPTER XXI THE TRIAL OF THE BOW ....- 89 -

CHAPTER XXII THE SLAYING OF THE SUITORS ....- 94 -

CHAPTER XXIII THE END OF THE WANDERING ....- 97 -

CHAPTER XXIV THE TRIUMPH OF ULYSSES ....- 100 -

INTRODUCTION

Three thousand years ago the world was still young. The western continent was a huge wilderness, and the greater part of Europe was inhabited by savage and wandering tribes. Only a few nations at the eastern end of the Mediterranean and in the neighbouring parts of Asia had learned to dwell in cities, to use a written language, to make laws for themselves, and to live in a more orderly fashion. Of these nations the most brilliant was that of the Greeks, who were destined in war, in learning, in government, and in the arts, to play a great part in the world, and to be the real founders of our modern civilization. While they were still a rude people, they had noble ideals of beauty and bravery, of duty and justice. Even before they had a written language, their singers had made songs about their heroes and their great deeds; and later these songs, which fathers had taught to children, and these children to their children, were brought together into two long and wonderful poems, which have ever since been the delight of the world, the *Iliad* and the *Odyssey*.

The *Iliad* is the story of the siege of Ilium, or Troy, on the western coast of Asia Minor. Paris, son of the king of Troy, had enticed Helen, the most beautiful of Grecian women, and the wife of a Grecian king, to leave her husband's home with him; and the kings and princes of the Greeks had gathered an army and a fleet and sailed across the Aegean Sea to rescue her. For ten years they strove to capture the city. According to the fine old legends, the gods themselves took a part in the war, some siding with the Greeks, and some with the Trojans. It was finally through Ulysses, a famous Greek warrior, brave and fierce as well as wise and crafty, that the Greeks captured the city.

The second poem, the *Odyssey*, tells what befell Ulysses, or Odysseus, as the Greeks called him, on his homeward way. Sailing from Troy with his little fleet of ships, which were so small that they used oars as well as sails, he was destined to wander for ten years longer before he could return to his rocky island of Ithaca, on the west shore of Greece, and to his faithful wife, Penelope.

He had marvellous adventures, for the gods who had opposed the Greeks at Troy had plotted to bring him ill-fortune. Just as his ships were safely rounding the southern cape of Greece, a fierce storm took them out of their course, and bore them to many strange lands—lands of giants, man-eating monsters, and wondrous enchantments of which you will delight to read. Through countless perils the resolute wanderer forced his way, losing ship after ship from his little fleet, and companion after companion from his own band, until he reached home friendless and alone, and found his palace, his property, and his family all in the power of a band of greedy princes. These he overcame by his cunning and his strength, and his long trials were ended.

As you read these ancient tales, you must forget what knowledge you have of the world, and think of it as the Greeks did. It was only a little part of the world that they knew at all,—the eastern end of the Mediterranean,— but even that seemed to them a great and marvellous region. Beyond its borders were strange and mysterious lands, in which wonders of all kinds were found, and round all ran the great world-river, the encircling stream of Ocean.

In the mountains of Olympus, to the northward, lived the gods. There was Zeus, greatest of all, the god of thunder and the wide heavens; Hera, his wife; Apollo, the archer god; Athene, the wise and clever goddess; Poseidon, who ruled the sea; Aphrodite, the goddess of love; Hephaestus, the cunning workman; Ares, the god of war; Hermes, the swift messenger; and others still, whom you will learn to know as you read. All these were worshipped by men with prayer and sacrifice; and, as in the early legends of many races, the gods often took the shape of men and women; they had their favourites and those whom they hated; and they ruled the fate of mortals as they chose.

If you let yourselves be beguiled into this old, simple way of regarding earth and heaven, you will not only love these ancient tales yourself, but you will see why, for century after century, they have been the longest loved and the best loved of all tales— beloved by old and young, by men and women and children. For they are hero-tales,—tales of war and adventure, tales of bravery and nobility, tales of the heroes that mankind, almost since the beginning of time, have looked to as ideals of wisdom and strength and beauty.

CHAPTER I
THE COUNSEL OF ATHENE

When the great city of Troy had been taken, all the chiefs who had fought against it set sail for their homes. But there was wrath in heaven against them, so that they did not find a safe and happy return. For one was shipwrecked, and another was shamefully slain by his false wife in his palace, and others found all things at home troubled and changed, and were driven to seek new dwellings elsewhere; and some were driven far and wide about the world before they saw their native land again. Of all, the wise Ulysses [Footnote: U-lys'-ses.] was he that wandered farthest and suffered most, for when ten years had well-nigh passed, he was still far away from Ithaca [Footnote: Ith'-a-ca.], his kingdom.

The gods were gathered in council in the hall of Olympus [Footnote: O-lym'-pus.], all but Poseidon, [Footnote: Po-sei'-don.] the god of the sea, for he had gone to feast with the Ethiopians. Now Poseidon was he who most hated Ulysses, and kept him from his home.

Then spake Athene among the immortal gods: "My heart is rent for Ulysses. Sore affliction doth he suffer in an island of the sea, where the daughter of Atlas keepeth him, seeking to make him forget his native land. And he yearns to see even the smoke rising up from the land of his birth, and is fain [Footnote: is fain, wishes to] to die. And thou regardest it not at all. Did he not offer thee many sacrifices in the land of Troy? Wherefore hast thou such wrath against him?" To her Zeus, the father of the gods, made reply: "What is this that thou sayest, my daughter? It is Poseidon that hath great wrath against Ulysses, because he blinded his son Polyphemus [Footnote: Pol-y-phe'-mus.] the Cyclops. [Footnote: Cy'-clops.] But come, let us take counsel together that he may return to his home, for Poseidon will not be able to contend against us all."

Then said Athene: "If this be thy will, then let us speed Hermes [Footnote: Her'-mes.] the messenger to the island of Calypso [Footnote: Ca-lyp'-so.], and let him declare to the goddess our purpose that Ulysses shall return to his home. And I will go to Ithaca, and stir up the spirit of his son Telemachus [Footnote: Te-lem'-a-chus.], that first he speak out his mind to the suitors of his mother who waste his substance, [Footnote: substance, property.] and next that he go to Sparta and to Pylos [Footnote: Py'-los.], seeking tidings of his father. So shall the youth win good report among men."

So she went to Ithaca, and there she took upon her the form of Mentes [Footnote: Men'-tes.], who was chief of the Taphians. [Footnote: Ta'-phi-ans.]

Now there were gathered in the house of Ulysses many princes from the islands, suitors of the Queen Penelope [Footnote: Pe-nel'-o- pe.], for they said that Ulysses was dead, and that she should choose another husband. These were gathered together, and were sitting playing draughts [Footnote: draughts, checkers.] and feasting. And Telemachus sat among them, vexed at heart, for they wasted his substance; neither was he master in his house. But when he saw the guest at the door, he rose from his place, and welcomed him, and made him sit down, and commanded that they should give him food and wine. And when he had ended his meal, Telemachus asked him his business.

Thereupon the false Mentes said: "My name is Mentes, and I am King of the Taphians, and I am sailing to Cyprus for copper, taking iron in exchange. Now I have been long time the friend of this house, of thy father and thy father's father, and I came trusting to see thy father, for they told me that he was here. But now I see that some god hath hindered his return, for that he is yet alive I know full well. But tell me, who are these that I see? Is this the gathering of a clan, or a wedding feast?"

Telemachus made answer: "O sir, while my father was yet alive, our house was rich and honoured; but now that he is gone, things are not well with me. I would not grieve so much had he fallen in battle before Troy; for then the Greeks would have built a great burial mound for him, and he would thus have won great renown, even for his son. But now the storms of the sea have swept him away, and I am left in sore distress. For these whom thou seest are the princes of the islands that come here to woo my mother. She neither refuseth nor accepteth; and meanwhile they sit here, and waste my substance."

Then said the false Mentes: "Now may the gods help thee! Thou art indeed in sore need of Ulysses. But now hearken to my counsel. First call an assembly of the people. Bid the suitors go back, each man to his home; and as for thy mother, if she be moved to wed, let her return to her father's house, that her kinsfolk may furnish a wedding feast, and prepare gifts such as a well-beloved daughter should have. Afterwards do thou fit up a ship with twenty oars, and go, inquire concerning thy father; perhaps some man may give thee tidings of him; or, may be, thou wilt hear a voice from Zeus concerning him. Go to Pylos first, and afterwards to Sparta, where Menelaus [Footnote: Me-ne-la'-us.] dwelleth, who of all the Greeks came back the last to his home. If thou shouldest hear that he is dead, then come back hither, and raise a mound for him, and give thy mother to a husband.

And when thou hast made an end of all these things, then plan how thou mayest slay the suitors by force or craft, for it is time for thee to have the thoughts of a man."

Then said Telemachus: "Thou speakest these things out of a friendly heart, as a father might speak to his son, nor will I ever forget them. But now, I pray thee, abide here for a space, that I may give thee a goodly gift, such as friends give to friends, to be an heirloom in thy house."

But the false Mentes said, "Keep me no longer, for I am eager to depart; give me thy gift when I shall return."

So the goddess departed; like to an eagle of the sea was she as she flew. And Telemachus knew her to be a goddess as she went.

Meanwhile Phemius [Footnote: Phe'-mi-us.] the minstrel sang to the suitors, and his song was of the unhappy return of the Greeks from Troy.

When Penelope heard the song, she came down from the upper chamber where she sat, and two handmaids bare her company. And when she came to where the suitors sat, she stood by the gate of the hall, holding her shining veil before her face. Then spake she to the minstrel, weeping, and said: "Phemius, thou knowest many songs concerning the deeds of gods and men; sing, therefore, one of these, and let the guests drink the wine in silence. But stay this pitiful strain, for it breaketh my heart to hear it. Surely, of all women I am the most unhappy, so famous was the husband for whom I mourn."

But Telemachus made reply: "Why dost thou grudge the minstrel, my mother, to make us glad in such fashion as his spirit biddeth him? It is no blame to him that he singeth of the unhappy return of the Greeks, for men most prize the song that soundeth newest in their ears. Endure, therefore, to listen, for not Ulysses only missed his return, but many a famous chief besides. Go, then, to thy chamber, and mind thy household affairs, and bid thy handmaids ply their tasks. Speech belongeth unto men, and chiefly to me that am the master in this house."

Then went she back to her chamber, for she was amazed at her son, with such authority did he speak. Then she bewailed her lord, till Athene sent down sleep upon her eyes.

When she was gone, Telemachus spake to the suitors, saying: "Let us now feast and be merry, and let there be no brawling among us. It is a good thing to listen to a minstrel that hath a voice as the voice of a god. But in the morning let us go to the assembly, that I may declare my purpose, to wit, that ye leave this hall, and eat your own substance. But if ye deem it a better thing that ye should waste another man's goods, and make no recompense, then work your will. But certainly Zeus shall repay you."

So he spake, and they all marvelled that he used such boldness. And Antinous [Footnote: An-ti'-no-us.] answered: "Surely, Telemachus, it is by the bidding of the gods that thou speakest so boldly. Therefore I pray that Zeus may never make thee King in Ithaca."

Then said Telemachus: "It is no ill thing to be a king, for his house groweth rich, and he himself is honoured. But there are others in Ithaca, young and old, who may have the kingship, now that Ulysses is dead. Yet know that I will be lord of my own house and of the slaves which Ulysses won for himself with his own spear."

Thereupon spake Eurymachus [Footnote: Eu-rym'-a-chus.], saying: "It is with the gods to say who shall be King in Ithaca; but no man can deny that thou shouldest keep thine own goods and be lord in thine own house. Tell me, who is this stranger that came but just now to thy house? Did he bring tidings of thy father? Or came he on some matter of his own? In strange fashion did he depart, nor did he tarry that we might know him."

Telemachus made answer: "Verily, Eurymachus, the day of my father's return hath gone by forever. As for this stranger, he said that he was Mentes, King of the Taphians."

So spake Telemachus, but in his heart he knew that the stranger was Athene. Then the suitors turned them to the dance and to the song, making merry till the darkness fell. Then went they each to his own house to sleep.

But Telemachus went to his chamber, pondering many things in his heart. And Eurycleia, [Footnote: Eu-ry-clei'-a] who had nursed him when he was little, went with him, bearing torches in her hands. He opened the door of the chamber, and took off his doublet, and put it in the wise woman's hands. She folded it, and smoothed it, and hung it on a pin, and went forth from the room, and pulled to the door, and made it fast. And all the night Telemachus thought in his heart of the journey which Athene had showed him.

CHAPTER II
THE ASSEMBLY

When the morning came, Telemachus bade the heralds call the people to the assembly. So the heralds called them, and they came in haste. And when they were gathered together, he went his way to the place of meeting, holding in his hand a spear, and two dogs followed him. Then did Athene shed a marvellous grace upon him, so that all men wondered at him, as he sat him down in his father's place.

First spake Aegyptus [Footnote: AE-gyp'-tus.], who was bowed with many years, and was very wise. Four sons he had. One had gone with Ulysses to Troy, and one was among the suitors of the Queen, and two abode with their father in the field. He said: "Hearken to me, men of Ithaca! Never hath an assembly been called in Ithaca since Ulysses departed. Who now hath called us together? If it be Telemachus, what doth he want? Hath he heard any tidings of the coming back of the host? He, methinks, is a true man. May Zeus be with him and grant him his heart's desire!"

So spake the old man, and Telemachus was glad at his speech. Then he rose up and said:—

"I have great trouble in my heart, men of Ithaca, for first my father, whom ye all loved, is dead; and next the princes of the islands come hither, making suit to my mother, but she waits ever for the return of her husband. And they devour all our substance; nor is Ulysses here to defend it, and I, in truth, am not able. And this is a grievous wrong, and not to be borne."

Then he dashed his sceptre on the ground, and sat down weeping. And Antinous, who was one of the suitors, rose up and said:—

"Nay, Telemachus, blame not us, but blame thy mother, who indeed is crafty above all women. For now this is the fourth year that we have come suing for her hand, and she has cheated us with hopes. Hear now this that she did. She set up a great web for weaving, and said to us: 'Listen, ye that are my suitors. Hasten not my marriage till I finish this web to be a burial cloth for Laertes [Footnote: La-er'-tes.], the father of Ulysses, for indeed it would be foul shame if he who has won great possessions should lack this honour.' So she spake, and for three years she cheated us, for what she wove in the day she unravelled at night. But when the fourth year was come, one of her maidens told us of the matter, and we came upon her by night and found her unravelling what she had woven in the day. Then did she finish it, much against her will. Send away, therefore, thy mother, and bid her marry whom she will. But till this be done we will not depart."

Then answered Telemachus: "How can I send away against her will her who bare me and brought me up? I cannot do this thing."

So he spake; and there came two eagles, which flew abreast till they came over the assembly. Then did they wheel in the air, and shook out from each many feathers, and tare each other, and so departed.

Then cried Alitherses [Footnote: A-li-ther'-ses.], the prophet: "Beware, ye suitors, for great trouble is coming to you, and to others also. And as for Ulysses, I said when he went to Troy that he should return after twenty years; and so it shall be."

And when the suitors would not listen, Telemachus said: "Give me a ship and twenty rowers, that I may go to Pylos and to Sparta; perhaps I may hear news of my father. And if I hear that he is dead, then will I come back hither and raise up a mound for him and give my mother to a husband."

Having thus spoken, he sat down, and Mentor [Footnote: Men'-tor.], whom Ulysses, when he departed, set over his household, rose up in the midst, and spake, saying: "Now henceforth never let any king be kind and gentle in his heart or minded to work righteousness. Let him rather be a hard man and unrighteous. For now no man of all the people whose lord he was remembereth Ulysses. Yet he was gentle as a father. If the suitors are minded to do evil deeds, I hinder them not. They do them at the peril of their own heads. It is with the people that I am wroth, to see how they sit speechless, and cry not shame upon the suitors; and yet they are many in number, and the suitors are few."

Then Leocritus [Footnote: Le-oc'-ri-tus.], who was one of the suitors, answered: "Surely thy wits wander, O Mentor, that thou biddest the people put us down. Of a truth, if Ulysses himself should come back, and should seek to drive the suitors from the hall, it would fare ill with him. An evil fate would he meet, if he fought with them. As for the people, let them go to their own houses. Let Mentor speed the young man's voyage, for he is a friend of his house. Yet I doubt whether he will ever accomplish it."

So he spake, and the assembly was dismissed.

But Telemachus went apart to the shore of the sea, and he washed his hands in the water of the sea, and prayed to Athene, saying: "Hear me, thou who didst come yesterday to the house, and bid me take a ship, and sail across the sea, seeking tidings of my father! The people delay my purpose, and the suitors stir them up in the wickedness of their hearts."

And while he prayed, Athene stood by him, like to Mentor in shape and speech. She spake, saying: "Thou art not without spirit, and art like to be a true son of Ulysses and Penelope. Therefore, I have good hopes that this journey of which thou speakest will not be in vain. But as for the suitors, think not of them, for they talk folly, and know not of the doom that is even now close upon them. Go, therefore, and talk with the suitors as before, and get ready food for a journey, wine and meal. And I will gather men who will offer themselves freely for the journey, and I will find a ship also, the best in Ithaca."

Then Telemachus returned to the house, and the suitors were flaying goats and singeing swine in the court. And Antinous caught him by the hand and said, "Eat and drink, Telemachus, and we will find a ship and rowers for thee, that thou mayest go where thou wilt, to inquire for thy father."

But Telemachus answered: "Think ye that I will eat and drink with you, who so shamefully waste my substance? Be sure of this, that I will seek vengeance against you, and if ye deny me a ship, I will even go in another man's."

So he spake, and dragged his hand from the hand of Antinous.

And another of the suitors said, "Now will Telemachus go and seek help against us from Pylos or from Sparta, or may be he will put poison in our cups, and so destroy us."

And another said: "Perchance he also will perish, as his father has perished. Then we should divide all his substance, but the house we should give to his mother and to her husband."

So they spake, mocking him. But he went to the chamber of his father, in which were ranged many casks of old wine, and gold and bronze, and clothing and olive oil; and of these things the prudent Eurycleia, who was the keeper of the house, had care. To her he spake: "Mother, make ready for me twelve jars of wine, not of the best, but of that which is next to it, and twenty measures of barley-meal. At even will I take them, when my mother sleeps, for I go to Pylos and Sparta; perchance I may hear news of my father."

But the old woman said, weeping: "What meanest thou, being an only son, thus to travel abroad? Wilt thou perish, as thy father has perished? For this evil brood of suitors will plot to slay thee and divide thy goods. Thou hadst better sit peaceably at home."

Then Telemachus said: "'Tis at the bidding of the gods I go. Only swear that thou wilt say naught to my mother till eleven or twelve days be past, unless, perchance, she should ask concerning me."

And the old woman sware that it should be so. And Telemachus went again among the suitors. But Athene, meanwhile, taking his shape, had gathered together a crew, and also had borrowed a ship for the voyage. And, lest the suitors should hinder the thing, she caused a deep sleep to fall upon them, so that they slept where they sat. Then she came in the shape of Mentor to the palace, and called Telemachus forth, saying:

"The rowers are ready; let us go."

Then Athene led the way, and they found the ship's crew upon the shore. To them spake Telemachus, saying, "Come now, my friends, let us carry the food on board, for it is all in the chamber, and no one knoweth of the matter; neither my mother, nor any of the maidens, but one woman only."

So they went to the house with him, and carried all the provision, and stowed it in the ship. Then Telemachus climbed the ship and sat down on the stern, and Athene sat by him.

And when he called to the crew, they made ready to depart. They raised the pine tree mast, and set it in the hole that was made for it, and they made it fast with stays. Then they hauled up the white sails with ropes of ox-hide. And the wind filled out the sail, and the water seethed about the stem of the ship, as she hasted through the water. And when all was made fast in the ship, then they mixed wine in the bowl, and poured out drink offerings to the gods, especially to Zeus.

So all the night, and till the dawn, the ship sped through the sea.

CHAPTER III
NESTOR

At sunrise the ship came to Pylos, where Nestor dwelt. Now it so chanced that the people were offering a great sacrifice upon the shore to Poseidon. Nine companies there were, and in each company five hundred men, and for the five hundred there were nine bulls. And they had tasted of the inner parts and were burning the slices of flesh on the thigh-bones to the god, when Telemachus's company moored the ship and came forth from it to the shore. Athene spake to Telemachus, saying: "Now thou hast no need to be ashamed. Thou hast sailed across the sea to hear tidings of thy father. Go, therefore, to Nestor, and learn what counsel he hath in the deep of his heart."

But Telemachus answered, "How shall I speak to him, being so untried and young?"

"Nay," said the goddess; "but thou shalt think of something thyself, and something the gods will put into thy mouth."

So saying she led the way, and they came to where Nestor sat, with his sons, and a great company round him, making ready the feast. When these saw the strangers, they clasped their hands, and made them sit down on soft fleeces of wool. And Nestor's son Peisistratus [Footnote: Pei-sis'-tra-tus] brought to them food, and wine in a cup of gold. To Athene first he gave the wine, for he judged her to be the elder of the two, saying, "Pray now to the Lord Poseidon, and make thy drink offering, and when thou hast so done, give the cup to thy friend that he may do likewise."

Then Athene took the cup and prayed to Poseidon, saying: "Grant renown to Nestor and his son, and reward the men of Pylos for this great sacrifice. And grant that we may accomplish that for which we have come hither."

And the son of Ulysses prayed in like manner.

When they had eaten and drunk their fill, Nestor said: "Strangers, who are ye? Sail ye over the seas for trade, or as pirates that wander at hazard of their lives?"

To him Telemachus made reply, Athene putting courage into his heart: "We come from Ithaca, and our errand concerns ourselves. I seek for tidings of my father, who in old time fought by thy side, and sacked the city of Troy. Of all the others who did battle with the men of Troy, we have heard, whether they have returned, or where they died; but even the death of this man remains untold. Therefore am I come hither to thee; perchance thou mayest be willing to tell me of him, whether thou sawest his death with thine own eyes, or hast heard it from another. Speak me no soft words for pity's sake, but tell me plainly what thou hast seen."

Nestor made answer: "Thou bringest to my mind all that we endured, warring round Priam's mighty town. There the best of us were slain. Valiant Ajax [Footnote: A'-jax.] lies there, and there Achilles [Footnote: A-chil'-les], and there Patroclus [Footnote: Pa-tro'-clus], and there my own dear son. Who could tell the tale of all that we endured? Truly, no one, not though thou shouldst abide here five years or six to listen. For nine whole years we were busy, devising the ruin of the enemy, which yet Zeus brought not to pass. And always Ulysses passed the rest in craft, thy father Ulysses, if indeed thou art his son, and verily thy speech is like to his; one would not think that a younger man could be so like to an elder. But listen to my tale. When we had sacked the town, I returned across the sea without delay, leaving behind the others, so that I know not of my own knowledge which of the Greeks was saved and which was lost. But wander not thou, my son, far from home, while strangers devour thy substance. Go to Menelaus, for he hath but lately come back from a far country; go and ask him to tell thee all that he knoweth. If thou wilt, go with thy ships, or, if it please thee better, I will send thee with a chariot and horses, and my sons shall be thy guides."

Then said Athene: "Let us cut up the tongues of the beasts, and mix the wine, and pour offerings to Poseidon and the other gods, and so bethink us of sleep, for it is the time."

So she spake, and they hearkened to her words. And when they had finished, Athene and Telemachus would have gone back to their ship. But Nestor stayed them, saying: "Now Zeus and all the gods forbid that ye should depart to your ships from my house, as though it were the dwelling of a needy man that hath not rugs and blankets in his house, whereon his guests may sleep! Not so; I have rugs and blankets enough. Never shall the son of my friend Ulysses lay him down on his ship's deck, while I am alive, or my children after me, to entertain strangers in my hall."

Thereupon said the false Mentor: "This is good, dear father. Let Telemachus abide with thee; but I will go back to the ship, and cheer the company, and tell them all. There I will sleep this night, and to-morrow I go to the Cauconians [Footnote: Cau-co'-ni- ans.], where there is owing to me a debt neither small nor of yesterday. But do thou send this man on his way in thy chariot."

Then the goddess departed in the semblance of a sea-eagle, and all that saw it were amazed.

Then the old man took Telemachus by the hand, and said: "No coward or weakling art thou like to be, whom the gods attend even now in thy youth. This is none other than Athene, daughter of Zeus, the same that stood by thy father in the land of Troy."

After this the old man led the company to his house. Here he mixed for them a bowl of wine eleven years old; and they prayed to Athene, and then lay down to sleep. Telemachus slept on a bedstead beneath the gallery, and Peisistratus slept by him.

The next day, as soon as it was morning, Nestor and his sons arose. And the old man said: "Let one man go to the plain for a heifer, and let another go to the ship of Telemachus, and bid all the company come hither, leaving two only behind. And a third shall command the goldsmith to gild the horns of the heifer, and let the handmaids prepare all things for a feast."

They did as the old man commanded; and after they had offered sacrifice, and had eaten and drunk, old Nester said, "Put now the horses in the chariot, that Telemachus may go his way."

So they yoked the horses, and the dame that kept the stores put into the chariot food and wine and dainties, such as princes eat. And Peisistratus took the reins, and Telemachus rode with him. And all that day they journeyed; and when the land grew dark they came to the city of Pherae [Footnote: Phe'-rae.], and there they rested; and the next day, travelling again, came to Lacedaemon [Footnote: La-ce-dae'-mon.], to the palace of King Menelaus.

CHAPTER IV
IN SPARTA

Now it chanced that Menelaus had made a great feast that day, for his daughter, the child of the fair Helen, was married to the son of Achilles, to whom she had been promised at Troy; and his son had also taken a wife. And the two wayfarers stayed their chariot at the door, and the steward spied them, and said to Menelaus:—

"Lo! here are two strangers who are like the children of kings. Shall we keep them here, or send them to another?"

But Menelaus was wroth, and said: "Shall we, who have eaten so often of the bread of hospitality, send these strangers to another? Nay, unyoke their horses and bid them sit down to meat." So the squires loosed the horses from the yoke, and fastened them in the stall, and gave them grain to eat and led the men into the hall. Much did they marvel at the sight, for there was a gleam as of the sun or moon in the palace of Menelaus. And when they had gazed their fill, they bathed them in the polished baths. After that they sat them down by the side of Menelaus. Then a handmaid bare water in a pitcher of gold, and poured it over a basin of silver that they might wash their hands. Afterwards she drew a polished table to their side, and a dame brought food, and set it by them, laying many dainties on the board, and a carver placed by them platters of flesh, and set near them golden bowls.

Then said Menelaus: "Eat and be glad; afterwards I will ask you who ye are, for ye seem like to the sons of kings."

And when they had ended the meal, Telemachus, looking round at the hall, said to his companion:—

"See the gold and the amber, and the silver and the ivory. This is like the hall of Zeus."

This he spake with his face close to his comrade's ear, but Menelaus heard him and said:—

"With the halls of the gods nothing mortal may compare. And among men also there may be the match of these things. Yet I have wandered far, and got many possessions in many lands. But woe is me! Would that I had but the third part of this wealth of mine, and that they who perished at Troy were alive again! And most of all I mourn for the great Ulysses, for whether he be alive or dead no man knows."

But Telemachus wept to hear mention of his father, holding up his purple cloak before his eyes. This Menelaus saw, and knew who he was, and pondered whether he should wait till he should himself speak of his father, or should rather ask him of his errand. But while he pondered there came in the fair Helen, and three maidens with her, of whom one set a couch for her to sit, and one spread a carpet for her feet, and one bare a basket of purple wool; but she herself had a distaff of gold in her hand. And when she saw the strangers she said:—

"Who are these, Menelaus? Never have I seen such likeness in man or woman as this one bears to Ulysses. Surely 'tis his son Telemachus, whom he left an infant at home when ye went to Troy for my sake!"

Then said Menelaus: "It must indeed be so, lady. For these are the hands and feet of Ulysses, and the look of his eyes and his hair. And but now, when I made mention of his name, he wept, holding his mantle before his face."

Then said Peisistratus: "King Menelaus, thou speakest truth. This is indeed the son of Ulysses who is come to thee; perchance thou canst help him by word or deed."

And Menelaus answered: "Then is he the son of a man whom I loved right well. I thought to give him a city in this land, bringing him from Ithaca with all his goods. Then should naught have divided us but death itself. But these things the gods have ordered otherwise."

At these words they all wept—the fair Helen and Telemachus and Menelaus; nor could Peisistratus refrain himself, for he thought of his dear brother who was slain at Troy.

Then said Menelaus: "Now we will cease from weeping; and to-morrow there is much that Telemachus and I must say one to the other."

Then the fair Helen put a mighty medicine in the wine whereof they drank—nepenthe [Footnote: ne-pen'-the], men call it. So mighty is it that whoever drinks of it, weeps not that day, though father and mother die, and though men slay brother or son before his eyes.

And after this she said: "It would take long to tell all the wise and valiant deeds of Ulysses. One thing, however, ye shall hear, and it is this: while the Greeks were before Troy he came into the city, having disguised himself as a beggar-man, yea, and he had laid many blows upon himself, so that he seemed to have been shamefully treated. I alone knew who he was, and questioned him, but he answered craftily. And I swore that I would not betray him. So he slew many Trojans with the sword, and learnt many things. And while other women in Troy lamented, I was glad, for my heart was turned again to my home."

Then Menelaus said: "Thou speakest truly, lady. Many men have I seen, and travelled over many lands, but never have I seen one who might be matched with Ulysses. Well do I remember how, when I and other chiefs of the Greeks sat in the horse of wood, thou didst come. Some god who loved the sons of Troy put the thing into thy heart. Thrice didst thou walk round our hiding-place and call by name to each one of the chiefs, speaking marvellously like his wife. Then would we have risen from our place or answered thee straightway. But Ulysses hindered us, and thus saved all the Greeks."

But Telemachus said: "Yet all these things have not kept him, for he has perished."

And after that they slept.

CHAPTER V
MENELAUS'S TALE

The next day Menelaus said to Telemachus: "For what end hast thou come hither to fair Lacedaemon?"

Then Telemachus said: "I have come to ask if thou canst tell me aught of my father. For certain suitors of my mother devour my goods, nor do I see any help. Tell me truly, therefore; knowest thou anything thyself about my father, or hast thou heard anything from another?"

And Menelaus answered:—

"In the river AEgyptus I was stayed long time, though I was eager to get home; the gods stayed me, for I had not offered to them due sacrifice. Now there is an island in the wash of the waves over against the land of Egypt—men call it Pharos [Footnote: Pha'- ros.], and it is distant one day's voyage for a ship, if the wind bloweth fair in her wake. Here did the gods keep me twenty days, nor did the sea winds ever blow. Then all my corn would have been spent, and the lives also of my men lost, if the daughter of Proteus [Footnote: Pro'-teus.]had not taken pity on me. Her heart was moved to see me when I wandered alone, apart from my company, for they all roamed about the island, fishing with hooks because hunger gnawed them. So she stood by me and spake, saying: 'Art thou foolish, stranger, and feeble of mind, or dost thou sit still for thine own pleasure, because it is sweet to thee to suffer? Verily, thou stayest long in this place, and canst find no escape, while the heart of thy people faileth within them.' Then I answered: 'I will tell thee the truth, whosoever thou art. It is not my own will that holdeth me here; I must have sinned against the gods. Tell me now which of the gods have I offended, and how shall I contrive to return to my own home?' So I spake, and straightway the goddess made answer: 'I will tell thee all. To this place comes Proteus, my father, who knoweth the depths of all the sea. If thou canst lay an ambush for him and catch him, he will declare to thee thy way, and tell thee how thou mayest return across the deep.' So she spake, and I made reply, 'Plan for me this ambush, lest by any chance he see me first and avoid me, for it is hard for a man to overcome a god.' Then said the goddess: 'When the sun in his course hath reached the midheaven, then cometh the old man from the sea; before the breath of the west wind he cometh, and the ripple covereth him. And when he is come out of the sea, he lieth down in the caves to sleep, and all about him lie the seals, the brood of ocean, and bitter is the smell of the salt water that they breathe. Thither will I lead thee at break of day, thee and three of thy companions. Choose them from thy ships, the bravest that thou hast. And now I will tell thee the old man's ways. First, he will count the seals, and then will lie down in the midst, as a shepherd in the midst of his flock. Now, so soon as ye shall see him thus laid down, then remember your courage, and hold him there. And he will take all manner of shapes of creatures that creep upon the earth, and of water likewise, and of burning fire. But do ye grasp him fast, and press him hard, and when he shall return to his proper shape, then let him go free, and ask him which of the gods is angry with thee, and how thou mayest return across the deep.' Thereupon she dived beneath the sea, and I betook me to the ships; but I was sorely troubled in heart. The next morning I took three of my comrades, in whom I trusted most, and lo! she had brought from the sea the skins of four sea-calves, which she had newly flayed, for she was minded to lay a snare for her father. She scooped hiding-places for us in the sand, and made us lie down therein, and cast the skin of a sea-calf over each of us. It would have been a grievous ambush, for the stench of the skins had distressed us sore,—who, indeed, would lay him down by a beast of the sea?—but she wrought a deliverance for us. She took ambrosia [Footnote: ambrosia, the food of the gods.], very sweet, and put it under each man's nostrils, that it might do away with the stench of the beast.

"So all the morning we waited with steadfast hearts. And the seals came forth from the brine, and ranged them in order upon the shore. And at noon the old man came forth out of the sea, and went along the line of the sea-beasts, and counted them. Us, too, he counted among them, and perceived not our device; and after that he laid him down to sleep. Then we rushed upon him with a cry, and held him fast; nor did he forget his cunning, for he became a bearded lion, and a snake, and a leopard, and a great wild boar. Also he took the shape of running water, and of a flowering tree. And all the while we held him fast. When at last he was weary, he said, 'Which of the gods, son of Atreus [Footnote: A'-treus.], bade thee thus waylay me?' But I answered him: 'Wherefore dost thou beguile me, old man, with crooked words? I am held fast in this isle, and can find no escape therefrom. Tell me now which of the gods hindereth me, and how I may return across the sea?' The old man made reply: 'Thou shouldst have done sacrifice to Zeus and the other gods before embarking, if thou wouldst have reached thy native country with speed. But now thou must go again to the river AEgyptus, and make offerings to the gods; then they will grant that which thou desirest.' Then was my spirit broken within me, when I heard that I must cross again this weary way, but I said: 'Old man, I will do all thy bidding. But tell me now, I pray thee, did the other Greeks, whom Nestor and I left behind us in Troy, return safe to their homes, or perished any by an evil death on board of his ship or among his friends?' To this the old man made reply: 'Thou doest ill to ask such things, for thou wilt weep to hear them. Thy brother indeed escaped from the fates of the sea; but the storm-wind carried him to the land where Aegisthus dwelt. And when Agamemnon [Footnote: Ag-a-mem'-non.] set foot upon his native land, he kissed it, weeping hot tears, so glad was he to see it again. And Aegisthus set an ambush for him, and slew him and all his companions.' Then I wept sore, caring not to live any more. But the old man said: 'Weep not, son of Atreus, for there is no help in tears. Rather make haste to return, that thou mayest take vengeance on AEgisthus.'[Footnote: AE-gis'-thus.] So he spake, and my heart was comforted within me, and I said: 'There is yet another of whom I would fain hear. Is he yet alive, wandering on the deep, or is he dead? Speak, though it grieve me to hear.' Straightway the old man answered: 'It is the son of Laertes of whom thou speakest. Him I saw in an island, even in the dwelling of Calypso; and he was shedding great tears, because the nymph keeps him there by force, so that he may not come to his own country, for he hath neither ship nor comrades.' So spake Proteus, and plunged into the sea. The next day we went back to the river AEgyptus, the stream that is fed from heaven, and offered sacrifice to the gods. And I made a great burial mound for Agamemnon, my brother, that his name might not be forgotten among men. And when these things had been duly performed, I set sail, and came back to my own country, for the gods gave me a fair wind. But do thou tarry now in my halls. And when thou art minded to go, I will give thee a chariot and three horses with it, and a goodly cup also, from which thou mayest pour offerings to the gods."

To him Telemachus made reply: "Keep me not long, son of Atreus, for my company wait for me in Pylos, though indeed I would be content to stay with thee for a whole year, nor would any longing for my home come over me. And let any gift thou givest me be a thing for me to treasure. But I will take no horses to Ithaca. Rather let them stay here and grace thy home, for thou art lord of a wide plain where there is wheat and rye and barley. But in Ithaca there is no meadow land. It is a pasture land of goats, yet verily it is more pleasant to my eyes than as if it were a fit feeding-place for horses."

Then said Menelaus: "Thou speakest well, as becometh the son of thy father. Come, now, I will change the gifts. Of all the treasures in my house, I will give thee the goodliest, especially a bowl which the King of the Sidonians gave me. Of silver it is, and the lips are finished with gold."

Now it had been made known meanwhile to the suitors in Ithaca that Telemachus was gone upon this journey seeking his father, and the thing displeased them much. And after they had held counsel about the matter, it seemed best that they should lay an ambush against him, and should slay him as he came back to his home. So Antinous took twenty men and departed, purposing to lie in wait in the strait between Ithaca and Samos.[Footnote: Sa'-mos.]

Nor was this plan unknown to Penelope, for the herald Medon [Footnote: Me'-don.]had heard it, and he told her how Telemachus had gone seeking news of his father, and how the suitors purposed to slay him as he returned. And she called her women, old and young, and rebuked them, saying: "Wicked ye were, for ye knew that he was about to go, and did not rouse me from my bed. Surely I would have kept him, eager though he was, from his journey!"

Then said Eurycleia: "Slay me, if thou wilt, but I will hide nothing from thee. I knew his purpose, and I furnished him with such things as he needed. But he made me swear that I would not tell thee till the eleventh or the twelfth day was come. But go with thy maidens and make thy prayer to Athene that she will save him, from death; for this house is not altogether hated by the gods."

Then Penelope, having duly prepared herself, went with her maidens to the upper chamber, and prayed aloud to Athene that she would save her son. And the suitors heard her praying, and said, "Surely the Queen prays, thinking of her marriage, nor knows that death is near to her son."

Then she lay down to sleep, and while she slept Athene sent her a dream in the likeness of her sister. And the vision stood over her head and spake: "Sleepest thou, Penelope? The gods would not have thee grieve, for thy son shall surely return."

And Penelope said: "How camest thou here, my sister? For thy dwelling is far away. And how can I cease to weep when my husband is lost? And now my son is gone, and I am sore afraid for him, lest his enemies slay him."

But the vision answered: "Fear not at all; for there is a mighty helper with him, even Athene, who hath bid me tell thee these things."

Then Penelope said: "If thou art a goddess, tell me this. Is my husband yet alive?"

But the vision answered, "That I cannot say, whether he be alive or dead." And so saying, it vanished into air.

And Penelope woke from her sleep, and her heart was comforted.

CHAPTER VI
ULYSSES ON HIS RAFT

Again the gods sate in council on high Olympus, and Athene spake among them, saying:

"Now let no king be minded to do righteously, for see how there is no man that remembereth Ulysses, who was as a father to his people. And he lieth far off, fast bound in Calypso's isle, and hath no ship to take him to his own country. Also the suitors are set upon slaying his son, who is gone to Pylos and to Lacedaemon, that he may get tidings of his father."

To her Zeus made answer: "What is this that thou sayest? Didst not thou thyself plan this in order that the vengeance of Ulysses might be wrought upon the suitors? As for Telemachus, guide him by thy skill, as well thou mayest, so that he may come to his own land unharmed, and the suitors may have their labour in vain."

Also he said to Hermes: "Hermes, go to the nymph Calypso, and tell her my sure purpose that Ulysses shall now come back to his home."

So Hermes put on his golden sandals, and took his wand in his hand, and came to the island of Ogygia [Footnote: O-gyg'-i-a.], and to the cave where Calypso dwelt. A fair place it was. In the cave was burning a fire of sweet-smelling wood, and Calypso sat at her loom, and sang with a lovely voice. And round about the cave was a grove of alders and poplars and cypresses, wherein many birds, falcons and owls and sea crows, were wont to roost; and all about the mouth of the cave was a vine with purple clusters of grapes; and there were four fountains which streamed four ways through meadows of parsley and violet. Very fair was the place, so that even a god might marvel at it, and Hermes stood and marvelled. Then went he into the cave, and Calypso knew him when she saw him face to face, for the gods know each other, even though their dwellings be far apart. But Ulysses was not there, for he sat, as was his wont, on the seashore, weeping and groaning, because he might not see wife and home and country.

Then Calypso said to Hermes: "Wherefore hast thou come hither, Hermes of the golden wand? Welcome thou art, but it is long since thou hast visited me. Tell me all thy thought, that I may fulfil it if I may, but first follow me, that I may set food before thee."

So she spread a table with ambrosia, and set it by him, and mixed the ruddy nectar [Footnote: nectar, the drink of the gods.] for him, and the messenger ate and drank. So, when he had comforted his soul with food, he spake, saying:—

"Thou questionest of my coming, and I will tell thee the truth. It is by no wish of mine own that I come, for who would of his free will pass over a sea so wide, wherein is no city of men that do sacrifice to the gods? Zeus bade me come, and none may go against the commands of Zeus. He saith that thou hast with thee a man more wretched than all his companions who fought against Troy for nine years and in the tenth year departed homeward. All the rest of his company were lost, but him the waves carried thither. Now, therefore, send him home with what speed thou mayest; for it is not fated that he should die away from his friends. He shall see again the high roof of his home and his native country."

It vexed Calypso much to hear this, for she would fain have kept Ulysses with her always, and she said:—

"Ye gods are always jealous when a goddess loves a mortal man. And as for Ulysses, did not I save him when Zeus had smitten his ship with a thunderbolt, and all his comrades had perished? And now let him go—if it pleases Zeus. Only I cannot send him, for I have neither ship nor rowers. Yet will I willingly teach him how he may safely return."

And Hermes said, "Do this thing speedily, lest Zeus be wroth with thee."

So he departed. And Calypso went seeking Ulysses, and found him on the shore of the sea, looking out over the waters, and weeping, for he was weary of his life, so much did he desire to see Ithaca again. She stood by him and said:—

"Weary not for thy native country, nor waste thyself with tears. If thou wilt go, I will speed thee on thy way. Take, therefore, thine axe and cut thee beams, and join them together, and make a deck upon them, and I will give thee bread and water and wine, and clothe thee also, so that thou mayest return safe to thy native country, for the gods will have it so."

"Nay," said Ulysses, "what is this that thou sayest? Shall I pass in a raft over the dreadful sea, over which even ships go not without harm? I will not go against thy will; but thou must swear the great oath of the gods that thou plannest no evil against me."

Then Calypso smiled and said: "These are strange words. I swear that I plan no harm against thee, but only such good as I would ask myself, did I need it; for indeed my heart is not of iron, but rather full of compassion."

Then they two went to the cave and sat down to meat, and she set before him food such as mortal men eat, but she herself ate ambrosia and drank nectar. And afterwards she said:—

"Why art thou so eager for thy home? Surely if thou knewest all the trouble that awaits thee, thou wouldst not go, but wouldst rather dwell with me. And though thou desirest all the day long to see thy wife, surely I am not less fair than she."

"Be not angry," Ulysses made reply. "The wise Penelope cannot, indeed, be compared to thee, for she is a mortal woman and thou art a goddess. Yet is my home dear to me, and I would fain see it again. Yea, and if some god should wreck me on the deep, yet would I endure it with patient heart. Already have I suffered much, and toiled much in perils of war and perils of the sea. And as to what is yet to come, let it be added to what hath been."

The next day Calypso gave him an axe with a handle of olive wood, and an adze, and took him to the end of the island, where there were great trees, long ago sapless and dry, alder and poplar and pine. Of these he felled twenty, and lopped them and worked them by the line. Then the goddess brought him an auger, and he made holes in the logs and joined them with pegs. And he made decks and side planking also; also a mast and a yard, and a rudder wherewith to turn the raft. And he fenced it about with a bulwark of willow twigs against the waves. The sails Calypso wove, and Ulysses fitted them with braces and halyards and sheets. Last of all he pushed the raft down to the sea with levers.

On the fourth day all was finished, and on the fifth day he departed. And Calypso gave him goodly garments, and a skin of wine, and a skin of water, and rich food in a bag of leather. She sent also a fair wind blowing behind, and Ulysses set his sails and proceeded joyfully on his way; nor did he sleep, but watched the stars, the Pleiades [Footnote: Plei'-a-des.] and Bootes [Footnote: Bo-o'-tes.], and the Bear, which turneth ever in one place, watching Orion.[Footnote: O-ri'-on.] For Calypso had said to him, "Keep the Bear ever on thy left as thou passest over the sea."

Seventeen days he sailed; and on the eighteenth day appeared the shadowy hills of the island of the Phaeacians. [Footnote: Phae-a'- ci-ans.] But now Poseidon, coming back from feasting with the Ethiopians, spied him as he sailed, and it angered him to the heart. He shook his head, and spake to himself, saying: "Verily, the gods must have changed their purpose concerning Ulysses while I was absent among the Ethiopians; and now he is nigh to the island of the Phaeacians, and if he reach it, he will escape from his woes. Yet even now I will send him far enough on a way of trouble."

Thereupon he gathered the clouds, and troubled the waters of the deep, holding his trident in his hand. And he raised a storm of all the winds that blow, and covered the land and the sea with clouds.

Sore troubled was Ulysses, and said to himself: "It was truth that Calypso spake when she said that I should suffer many troubles returning to my home. Would that I had died that day when many a spear was cast by the men of Troy over the dead Achilles. Then would the Greeks have buried me; but now shall I perish miserably."

And as he spake a great wave struck the raft and tossed him far away, so that he dropped the rudder from his hand. Nor for a long time could he rise, so deep was he sunk, and so heavy was the goodly clothing which Calypso had given him. Yet at the last he rose, and spat the salt water out of his mouth, and sprang at the raft, and caught it, and sat thereon, and was borne hither and thither by the waves. But Ino [Footnote: I'-no.] saw him and pitied him—a woman she had been, and was now a goddess of the sea,—and rose from the deep like to a sea-gull upon the wing, and sat upon the raft, and spake, saying:—

"Luckless mortal, why doth Poseidon hate thee so? He shall not slay thee, though he fain would do it. Put off these garments, and swim to the land of Phaeacia, putting this veil under thy breast. And when thou art come to the land, loose it from thee, and cast it into the sea."

Then the goddess gave him the veil, and dived again into the deep as a sea-gull diveth, and the waves closed over her. Then Ulysses pondered the matter, saying to himself: "Woe is me! can it be that another of the gods is contriving a snare for me, bidding me leave my raft? Verily, I will not yet obey her counsel, for the land, when I saw it, seemed a long way off. I am resolved what to do; so long as the raft will hold together, so long will I abide on it; but when the waves shall break it asunder, then will I swim, for nothing better may be done."

But while he thought thus within himself, Poseidon sent another great wave against the raft. As a stormy wind scattereth a heap of husks, so did the wave scatter the timbers of the raft. But Ulysses sat astride on a beam, as a man sitteth astride of a horse; and he stripped off from him the goodly garments which Calypso had given him, and put the veil under his breast, and so leapt into the sea, stretching out his hands to swim.

And Poseidon, when he saw him, shook his head, and said: "Even so go wandering over the deep, till thou come to the land. Thou wilt not say that thou hast not had trouble enough."

But Athene, binding up the other winds, roused the swift north wind, that so Ulysses might escape from death.

So for two days and two nights he swam. But on the third day there was a calm, and he saw the land from the top of a great wave, for the waves were yet high, close at hand. But when he came near he heard the waves breaking along the shore, for there was no harbour there, but only cliffs and rugged rocks.

Then at last the knees of Ulysses were loosened with fear, and his heart was melted within him, and in heaviness of spirit he spake to himself: "Woe is me! for now, when beyond all hope Zeus hath given me the sight of land, there is no place where I may win to shore from out of the sea. For the crags are sharp, and the waves roar about them, and the smooth rock riseth sheer from the sea, and the water is deep, so that I may gain no foothold. If I should seek to land, then a great wave may dash me on the rocks. And if I swim along the shore, to find some harbour, I fear lest the winds may catch me again and bear me out into the deep; or it may be that some god may send a monster of the sea against me; and verily there are many such in the sea-pastures, and I know that Poseidon is very wroth against me."

While he pondered these things in his heart a great wave bare him to the rocks. Then would his skin have been stripped from him and all his bones broken, had not Athene put a thought into his heart. For he rushed in towards the shore, and clutched the rock with both his hands, and clung thereto till the wave had passed. But as it ebbed back, it caught him, and carried him again into the deep. Even as a cuttle-fish is dragged from out its hole in the rock, so was he dragged by the water, and the skin was stripped from his hand against the rocks. Then would Ulysses have perished, if Athene had not put a plan in his heart. He swam outside the breakers, along the shore, looking for a place where the waves might be broken, or there should be a harbour. At last he came to where a river ran into the sea. Free was the place of rocks, and sheltered from the wind, and Ulysses felt the stream of the river as he ran. Then he prayed to the river-god:—

"Hear me, O King, whosoever thou art. I am come to thee, fleeing from the wrath of Poseidon. Save me, O King."

Thereupon the river stayed his stream, and made the water smooth before Ulysses, so that at last he won his way to the land. His knees were bent under him, and his hands dropped at his side, and the salt water ran out from his mouth and nostrils. Breathless was he, and speechless; but when he came to himself, he loosed the veil from under his breast, and cast it into the salt stream of the river and the stream bare it to the sea, and Ino came up and caught it in her hands.

Then he lay down on the rushes by the bank of the river and kissed the earth, thinking within himself: "What now shall I do? for if I sleep here by the river, I fear that the dew and the frost may slay me; for indeed in the morning-time the wind from the river blows cold. And if I go up to the wood, to lay me down to sleep in the thicket, I fear that some evil beast may devour me."

But it seemed better to go to the wood. So he went. Now this was close to the river, and he found two bushes, one of wild olive, and the other of fruitful olive. So thickly grown together were they that the winds blew not through them, nor did the sun pierce them, nor yet the rain. Ulysses crept thereunder, and found a great pile of leaves, shelter enough for two or three, even in winter time, when the rain is heavy. Then did Ulysses rejoice, laying himself in the midst, and covering himself with leaves. And Athene sent down upon his eyelids deep sleep, that might ease him of his toil.

CHAPTER VII
NAUSICAA

Meanwhile Athene went to the city of Phaeacians, to the palace of Alcinous [Footnote: Al-cin'-o-us.], their King. There she betook her to the chamber where slept Nausicaa, daughter of the King, a maiden fair as are the gods. The goddess stood above the maiden, in the likeness of a girl that was of equal age with her, and had found favour in her sight.

Athene spake, saying: "Why hath thy mother so careless a child, Nausicaa? Lo! thy raiment lieth unwashed, and yet the day of thy marriage is at hand, when thou must have fair clothing for thyself, and to give to them that shall lead thee to thy bridegroom's house; for thus doth a bride win good repute. Do thou therefore arise with the day, and go to wash the raiment, and I will go with thee. Ask thy father betimes in the morning to give thee mules and a wagon to carry the raiment and the robes. Also it is more becoming for thee to ride than to go on foot, for the washing places are far from the city."

And when the morning was come, Nausicaa awoke, marvelling at the dream, and went seeking her parents. Her mother she found busy with her maidens at the loom, spinning yarn dyed with purple of the sea, and her father she met as he was going to the council with the chiefs of the land. Then she said: "Give me, father, the wagon with the mules, that I may take the garments to the river to wash them. Thou shouldest always have clean robes when thou goest to the council; and there are my five brothers also, who love to have newly washed garments at the dance."

But of her own marriage she said nothing. And her father, knowing her thoughts, said: "I grudge thee not, dear child, the mules or aught else. The men shall harness for thee a wagon with strong wheels and fitted also with a frame."

Then he called to the men, and they made ready the wagon, and harnessed the mules; and the maiden brought the raiment out of her chamber, and put it in the wagon. Also her mother filled a basket with all manner of food, and poured wine in a goat-skin bottle. Olive oil also she gave her, that Nausicaa and her maidens might anoint themselves after the bath. And Nausicaa took the reins, and touched the mules with the whip. Then was there a clatter of hoofs, and the mules went on with their load, nor did they grow weary.

When they came to the river, where was water enough for the washing of raiment, the maidens loosed the mules from the chariot, and set them free to graze in the sweet clover by the river-bank. Then they took the raiment from the wagon, and bare it to the river, and trod it in the trenches. And when they had cleansed all the garments, they laid them on the shore of the sea, where the waves had washed the pebbles clean. After that they bathed, and anointed themselves; and then they sat down to eat and drink by the river-side; and after the meal they played at ball, singing as they played, and Nausicaa led the song. And Nausicaa was fairer than all the maidens. And when they had ended their play, and were yoking the mules, and folding up the raiment, then Athene contrived that the princess, throwing the ball to one of her maidens, cast it so wide that it fell into the river. Thereupon they all cried aloud, and Ulysses awoke. And he said to himself: "What is this land to which I have come? Are they that dwell therein fierce or kind to strangers? Just now I seemed to hear the voice of nymphs [Footnote: nymphs, spirits of the woods and waters], or am I near the dwellings of men?"

Then he twisted a leafy bough about his loins, and rose up and went towards the maidens, who were frightened to see him (for he was wild-looking), and fled hither and thither. But Nausicaa stood and fled not. Then Ulysses cried, saying:—

"O Queen, whether thou art a goddess, I know not. But if thou art a mortal, happy are thy father and mother, and happy thy brothers, and happiest of all he who shall win thee in marriage. Never have I seen man or woman so fair. Thou art like a young palm tree that but lately I saw springing by the temple of the god. But as for me, I have been cast on this shore, having come from the island of Ogygia. Pity me, then, and lead me to the city, and give me something, a wrapper of this linen, maybe, to put about me. So may the gods give thee all blessings!"

And Nausicaa made answer: "Thou seemest, stranger, to be neither evil nor foolish. Thou shalt not lack clothing or food, and I will take thee to the city. Know also that this land is Phaeacia, and that I am daughter to Alcinous, who is king thereof."

Then she called to her maidens: "What mean ye to flee when ye see a man? No enemy comes hither to harm us, for we are dear to the gods, and also we live in an island of the sea, so that men may not approach to work us wrong. If one cometh here overcome by trouble, it is well to help him. Give this man, therefore, food and drink, and wash him in the river, where there is shelter from the wind."

So they brought him down to the river, and gave him clothing, and also olive-oil in a flask of gold. Then, at his bidding, they departed a little space, and he washed the salt from his skin and out of his hair, and anointed himself, and put on the clothing. And Athene made him taller and fairer to see, and caused the hair to be thick on his head, in colour as a hyacinth. Then he sat down on the seashore, right beautiful to behold, and the maiden said:—

"Not without the bidding of the gods comes this man to our land. Before, indeed, I deemed him uncomely, but now he seems like to the gods. I should be well content to have such a man for a husband, and maybe he might will to abide in this land. Give him, ye maidens, food and drink."

So they gave him, and he ate ravenously, having fasted long. Then Nausicaa bade yoke the mules, and said to Ulysses:—

"Arise, stranger, come with me, that I may bring thee to the house of my father. But do thou as I shall tell thee. So long as we shall be passing through the fields, follow quickly with the maidens behind the chariot. But when we shall come to the city, —thou wilt see a high wall and a harbour on either side of the narrow way that leadeth to the gate,—then follow the chariot no more. Hard by the wall is a grove of Athene, a grove of poplars, with a spring in the midst, and a meadow round about; there abide till I have reached the house of my father. For I would not that the people should speak lightly of me. And I doubt not that were thou with me some one would say: 'Who is this stranger, tall and fair, that cometh with Nausicaa? Will he be her husband? Perchance it is some god who has come down at her prayer, or a man from far away; for she scorns us men of Phaeacia.' It would be a shame that such words should be spoken. But when thou shalt judge that I have come to the palace, then go up thyself and ask for my father's house. Any one, even a child, can show it thee, for the other Phaeacians dwell not in such. And when thou art come within the doors, pass quickly through the hall to where my mother sits. Close to the hearth is her seat, and my father's hard by, where he sits with the wine-cup in his hand as a god. Pass him by, and kneel to my mother, and pray her that she give thee safe return to thy country."

Then she smote the mules with the whip. Quickly did they leave the river behind them; but the maiden was heedful to drive them so that Ulysses and the maidens might be able to follow on foot. At sunset they came to the sacred grove of Athene, and there Ulysses sat him down, and prayed to Athene, saying, "Hear me, now, O daughter of Zeus, and grant that this people may look upon me with pity."

So he spake, and Athene heard him, but showed not herself to him, face to face, for she feared the wrath of her uncle Poseidon.

CHAPTER VIII
ALCINOUS

Nausicaa came to her father's house, and there her brothers unyoked the mules from the wagon, and carried the garments into the house; and the maiden went to her chamber, where a nurse kindled for her a fire, and prepared a meal.

At the same time Ulysses rose to go to the city; and Athene spread a mist about him, for she would not that any of the Phaeacians should see him and mock him. And when he was now about to enter the city, the goddess took upon herself the shape of a young maiden carrying a pitcher, and met him.

Then Ulysses asked her: "My child, canst thou tell me where dwells Alcinous? for I am a stranger in this place."

She answered: "I will show thee, for he dwells near to my own father. But be thou silent, for we Phaeacians love not strangers over much."

Then Athene led the way, and Ulysses followed after her; and much he marvelled, as he went, at the harbours, and the ships, and the places of assembly, and the walls. And when they came to the palace, Athene said: "This is the place for which thou didst inquire. Enter in; here thou shalt find kings at the feast; but be not afraid; the fearless man ever fares the best. And look thou first for Queen Arete.[Footnote: A-re'-te.] If she be well disposed to thee, doubtless thou wilt see thy native country again."

Having thus spoken, Athene departed, and Ulysses entered the palace. In it there was a gleam as of the sun or the moon.

A wondrous place it was, with walls of brass and doors of gold, hanging on posts of silver; and on either side of the door were dogs of gold and silver, and against the wall, all along from the threshold to the inner chamber, were set seats, on which sat the chiefs of the Phaeacians, feasting; and youths wrought in gold stood holding torches in their hands, to give light in the darkness. Fifty women were in the house, grinding corn and weaving robes, for the women of the land are no less skilled to weave than are the men to sail the sea. And round about the house were beautiful gardens, with orchards of fig, and apple, and pear, and pomegranate, and olive. Drought hurts them not, nor frost, and harvest comes after harvest without ceasing. Also there was a vineyard; and some of the grapes were parching in the sun, and some were being gathered, and some again were but just turning red. And there were beds of all manner of flowers; and in the midst of all were two fountains which never failed.

These things Ulysses regarded for a space, and then passed into the hall. And there the chiefs of Phaeacia were drinking their last cup to Hermes. Quickly he passed through them, and put his hands on the knees of Arete and said—and as he spake the mist cleared from about him, and all that were in the hall beheld him:—

"I implore thee, and thy husband, and thy guests, to send me home to my native country. The gods bless thee and them, and grant you to live in peace, and that your children should come peacefully after you!"

And he sat down in the ashes of the hearth. Then for a space all were silent, but at the last spake Echeneus [Footnote: E-che-ne'- us.], who was the oldest man in the land:—

"King Alcinous, this ill becomes you that this man should sit in the ashes of the hearth. Raise him and bid him sit upon a seat, and let us pour out an offering to Father Zeus, who is the friend of strangers, and let the keeper of the house give him meat and drink."

And Alcinous did so, bidding his eldest born, Laodamas [Footnote: La-o'-da-mas.], rise from his seat. And an attendant poured water on his hands, and the keeper of the house gave him meat and drink. Then, when all had poured out an offering to Father Zeus, King Alcinous spake, saying: "In the morning we will call an assembly of the people, and consider how we may take this stranger to his home, so that he may reach it without trouble or pain. Home will we take him without hurt, but what things may befall him there, we know not; these shall be as the Fates spun his thread. But, if he is a god and not a man, then is this a new device of the gods. For heretofore they have shown themselves openly in our midst, when we offer sacrifice, and sit by our sides at feasts. Yea, and if a traveller meet them on the way, they use no disguise, for indeed they are near of kin to us."

Then spake Ulysses: "Think not such things within thy heart, O King! I am no god but one that is most miserable among the sons of men. Of many woes might I tell. Nevertheless, suffer me to eat; for, however sad a man may be, yet he must eat and drink. But when the day cometh, bestir yourselves, and carry me to my home. Fain would I die if I could see my home again!"

And they answered that it should be so, and went each to his home. Only Ulysses was left in the hall, and Alcinous and Arete with him. And Arete recognized his clothing, and said:—

"Whence art thou, stranger? and who gave thee these garments?"

So Ulysses told her how he had come from the island of Calypso, and what he had suffered, and how Nausicaa had found him on the shore, and had guided him to the city.

And Alcinous blamed the maiden because she had not herself brought him to the house. "Nay," said Ulysses, "she would have brought me, but I would not, fearing thy wrath." For he would not have the maiden blamed.

Then said Alcinous: "I am not one to be angered for such cause. Gladly would I have such a one as thou art to be my son-in-law, and I would give him house and wealth. But no one would I hold against his will. As for sending thee to thy home, that is easy; thou shalt lay thee down to sleep, and my men shalt smite the sea with oars, and take thee whithersoever thou wilt, even though it be to the furthest of all lands. For verily my ships are the best that sail the sea, and my young men the most skilful of all that ply the oar."

So he spake, and Ulysses rejoiced to hear his words. And he prayed within himself, "Grant, Father Zeus, that Alcinous may fulfil all that he hath said, and that I may come to my own land!"

Then Arete bade her handmaids prepare a bed for the stranger. So they went from the hall, with torches in their hands, and made it ready. And when they had ended they called Ulysses, saying, "Up, stranger, and sleep, for thy bed is ready."

Right glad was he to sleep after all that he had endured.

CHAPTER IX
THE PHAEACIANS

The next day the King arose at dawn, as also did Ulysses, and the King led the way to the place of assembly. Meanwhile Athene, wearing the guise of the King's herald, went throughout the city, and to each man she said, "Come to the assembly, captains and counsellors of the Phaeacians, that ye may learn concerning this stranger, who hath lately come to the hall of Alcinous."

So she roused their desire, and the place of assembly was filled to the utmost; much did the men marvel to see Ulysses, for Athene had poured marvellous grace upon him, making him fairer and taller and stronger to see.

Then the King rose up and spake: "Hearken, captains and counsellors of the people, to what I say. This stranger hath come to my hall; I know not who he is or whence he comes, whether it be from the rising or the setting of the sun; and he prays that he may be safely carried to his home. Let us therefore choose a ship that hath never sailed before, and two and fifty youths that are the best to ply the oar; and when ye have made ready the ship, then come to my house and feast; I will provide well for all. Bid. also, Demodocus [Footnote: De-mod'-o-cus.] the minstrel to come, for the gods have given to him above all others the gift of song wherewith to rejoice the hearts of men."

Then they did as the King counselled. They made ready the ship, and moored her by the shore, and after that they went to the palace of the King. From one end thereof to the other it was crowded, for many were there, both young and old. And Alcinous slew for them twelve sheep, and eight swine, and two oxen; and his men prepared for the people a goodly feast.

Then came the servants of the King, leading the blind minstrel by the hand. The servants set him in a silver chair, in the midst of the guests, and hung a harp above his head, and showed him how he might reach his hand to take it. And close by his side they placed a table and a basket and a cup of wine, that he might drink at his pleasure.

So the Phaeacians feasted in the hall; and when they had had enough of meat and drink, then the minstrel sang. He sang a song, the fame of which had reached to heaven, of the quarrel between Ulysses and Achilles, when they were fighting to capture Troy.

But as the minstrel sang, Ulysses held his purple cloak before his face, for he was ashamed to weep in the sight of the people. Whensoever the singer ceased from his song, then did Ulysses wipe away the tears; but when he began again, for the chiefs loved to hear the song, then again he covered his face and wept. But none noted the thing but Alcinous.

Then the King said to the chiefs, "Now that we have feasted and delighted ourselves with song, let us go forth, that this stranger may see that we are skilful in boxing and wrestling and running."

Then stood up many Phaeacian youths, and the fairest and strongest of them all was Laodamas, eldest son to the King, and they ran a race, and wrestled, and threw quoits, and leaped.

Then Laodamas said to Ulysses, "Wilt thou not try thy skill in some game, and put away the trouble from thy heart?"

But Ulysses answered: "Why askest thou this? I think of my troubles rather than of sport, and care only that I may see again my home."

Then said another: "And in very truth, stranger, thou hast not the look of a wrestler or boxer. Rather would one judge thee to be some trader, who sails over the sea for gain."

"Nay," answered Ulysses, "this is ill said. True it is that the gods give not all gifts to all men, beauty to one, and sweet speech to another. Fair of form art thou; no god could better thee; but thou speakest idle words. I am not unskilled in these things, but stood among the first in the old days; but since have I suffered much in battle and shipwreck. Yet will I make trial of my strength, for thy words have angered me."

Whereupon, clad in his mantle as he was, he took a quoit, heavier far than such as the Phaeacians were wont to throw, and sent it with a whirl. It flew through the air, so that the brave Phaeacians crouched to the ground in fear, and it fell far beyond all the rest.

Then Athene, for she had taken upon herself the guise of a Phaeacian man, marked the place where it fell, and spake, saying: "Stranger, verily, even a blind man might find this token of thy strength, for it is not lost among the others, but lies far beyond them. Be of good courage, therefore, in this contest; none of the Phaeacians shall surpass thee."

Then was Ulysses glad, seeing that he had a friend among the people, and he said: "Now match this throw, young men, if ye can. Soon will I cast another after it, as far, or further yet. And, if any man is so minded, let him rise up and contend with me, for I will match myself in wrestling or boxing, or even in the race, with any man in Phaeacia, save Laodamas only, for he is my friend. I can shoot with the bow; and I can cast a spear as far as other men can shoot an arrow. But as for the race, it may be that some one might outrun me, for I have suffered much on the sea."

But they were all silent, till the King stood up and said: "Thou hast spoken well. But we men of Phaeacia are not mighty to wrestle or to box; only we are swift of foot and skilful to sail upon the sea. And we love feasts, and dances, and the harp, and gay clothing, and the bath. In these things no man may surpass us."

Then the King bade Demodocus the minstrel to sing again. And when he had done so, the King's two sons danced together; and afterwards they played with the ball, throwing it into the air, cloud high, and catching it right skilfully.

And afterwards the King said: "Let us each give this stranger a mantle and a tunic and a talent of gold."

Then all the princes brought their gifts. And Alcinous said to the Queen: "Lady, bring hither a chest, the best that thou hast, and put therein a robe and a tunic. And I will give our guest a fair golden cup of my own, that he may remember me all the days of his life, when he poureth out offerings to the gods."

Then the Queen brought from her chamber a fair chest, and put therein the gifts which the princes had given; also with her own hands she put therein a robe and a tunic. And she said:—

"Look now to the lid, and tie a knot, that no man rob thee by the way, when thou sleepest in the ship."

So Ulysses fixed well the lid, and tied it with a cunning knot which Circe had taught him. After that he went to the bath. As he came from the bath Nausicaa met him by the entering in of the hall, and marvelled at him, so fair was he to look upon. And she spake, saying: "Stranger, farewell. But when thou comest to thine own country, think upon me once and again, for indeed thou owest to me the price of thy life."

Ulysses made answer to her, "Nausicaa, if Zeus grant me safe return to my home, I will do honour to thee as to a goddess, forever; for indeed I owe thee my life."

Then he went into the hall, and sat down by the side of the King, and the squire came leading the blind minstrel by the hand. Now Ulysses had cut off a rich portion from the chine [Footnote: chine, backbone.] of a boar that had been set before him, and he said to the squire: "Take this and give it to Demodocus, for the minstrel should be held in honour by men."

So the squire bare the dish, and set it on the knees of the minstrel, rejoicing his heart.

When they all had had enough of food and drink, then Ulysses spake to the minstrel, saying: "Demodocus, I know not whether the gods have taught thee, but of a truth thou singest of all the toil and trouble that the Greeks endured before the great city of Troy as if thou hadst thyself been there. Come, now, sing to us of the Horse of Wood, and how Ulysses contrived that it should be taken up into the citadel of Troy when he had filled it with the bravest of the chiefs. Sing me this aright, and I will bear witness for thee that thou art indeed a minstrel whom the gods have taught."

Then did the minstrel sing this song. He told how one part of the Greeks set fire to their camp, and embarked upon their ships, and sailed away; and how the other part—Ulysses and his comrades—sat hidden in the Horse which the men of Troy had dragged with their own hands into their place of assembly. All about sat the people, and three counsels were given. The first was to cleave the wood, and the second to drag it to the brow of the hill and cast it down thence, and the third to leave it as an offering to the gods; and the third counsel prevailed, for it was the doom of the city that it should perish through the Horse.

Also the minstrel sang how the chiefs came forth from the Horse, and went through the city, wasting it; and much also of Ulysses and his brave deeds.

Thus did the minstrel sing, and the heart of Ulysses was melted within him as he listened, and the tears ran down his cheeks.

But none of the company, save King Alcinous only, noticed this. Then the King spake, saying: "Hearken, ye princes of the Phaeacians, and let Demodocus cease from his singing, for since he set his hand to the harp, this stranger hath not ceased to weep. Let, therefore, the minstrel cease, and let us make merry and rejoice as it is fitting to do. Are we not met together that we may give gifts to this stranger, and send him to his home? And hide not thou, stranger, from us aught that I shall ask thee. Tell us by what name they call thee at home, for no man lacketh a name. Tell us also of thy land and thy city, that our ships may shape their course to take thee thither. For these are not as the ships of other men, that have steersmen and rudders. They have an understanding of their own, and know all the cities of men, and they pass over the deep, covered with cloud, and have no fear of wreck. But my father was wont to say that Poseidon bore a grudge against us because we carry all men safely to their homes; and that one day he would smite a ship of ours as it came home from such an errand, changing it to a rock that should overshadow our city. But thou, stranger, tell us of thyself,

—whither thou hast wandered, and what cities thou hast seen, be they cities of the unrighteous, or cities of them that are hospitable to strangers and fear the gods. Tell us, too, why thou didst weep at hearing of the tale of Troy. Hadst thou, perchance, a kinsman, or a friend— for a wise friend is ever as a brother—among those that perished at Troy?"

CHAPTER X
THE CYCLOPS

(THE TALE OF ULYSSES)

Then Ulysses answered the King, saying: "What shall I tell thee first, and what last, for many sorrows have the gods laid upon me? First, I will tell my name, that ye may know it, and that there may be friendship between us, even when I shall be far away. I am ULYSSES, SON OF LAERTES. In Ithaca I dwell. Many islands lie about it, but Ithaca is furthest to the west, and the others face the sun-rising. Very rugged is this island of Ithaca, but it is the mother of brave men; verily, there is nothing dearer to a man than his own country. Calypso, the fair goddess, would have had me abide with her, to be her husband; but she did not prevail, because there is nothing that a man loves more than his country and his parents. But now I will tell thee of all the troubles that the gods laid upon me as I journeyed from Troy.

"The wind that bare me from Troy brought me to Ismarus [Footnote: Is'-ma-rus.], which is a city of the Cicones.[Footnote: Ci'-co- nes.] This I sacked, slaying the people that dwelt therein. But the people of the city fetched their kinsmen that dwelt in the mountains, and they overcame us, and drave us to our ships. Six from each ship perished, but the remainder of us escaped from death.

"Then we sailed, stricken with grief for our dear comrades, yet rejoicing that we had escaped from destruction. When we had sailed a little space, Zeus sent the north wind against us with a mighty storm, covering with clouds both land and sea, and the ships were driven before it. So we lowered the sails, and rowed the ships to the land with all our might. For two days we endured much distress and sorrow, but on the third, when the morning light appeared, we hoisted the sails and rested. Then I should have come to my own country, but the north wind and the sea drave me from my course. For nine days did the wind carry us before it.

"And on the tenth day we came to the land where the lotus grows—a wondrous fruit, for whoever eats of it cares not to see country or wife or children again. Now the Lotus-eaters, for so the people of the land are called, were a kindly folk, and gave of the fruit to some of the sailors, not meaning them any harm, but thinking it to be the best that they had to give. These, when they had eaten, said that they would not sail any more over the sea; and, when I heard this, I bade their comrades bind them and carry them, sadly complaining, to the ships.

"Then, the wind having abated, we took to our oars, and rowed for many days till we came to the country where the Cyclopes [Footnote: Cy-clo'-pes.] dwell. Now a mile or so from the shore there was an island, very fair and fertile, but no man dwells there or tills the soil, and in the island a harbour where a ship may be safe from all winds, and at the head of the harbour a stream falling from a rock, and whispering alders all about it. Into this the ships passed safely, and were hauled up on the beach, and the crews slept by them, waiting for the morning.

"When the dawn appeared, we wandered through the island; and the Nymphs of the land started the wild goats, that my company might have food to eat. Thereupon we took our bows and our spears from the ships, and shot at the goats; and the gods gave us plenty of prey. Twelve ships I had in my company, and each ship had nine goats for its share, and my own portion was ten.

"Then all the day we sat and feasted, drinking sweet wine which we had taken from the city of the Cicones, and eating the flesh of the goats; and as we sat we looked across to the land of the Cyclops, seeing the smoke and hearing the voices of the men and of the sheep and of the goats. And when the sun set and darkness came over the land, we lay down upon the seashore and slept.

"The next day I gathered my men together, and said, 'Abide ye here, dear friends; I with my own ship and my own company will go and find whether the folk that dwell in yonder island are just or unjust.'

"So I climbed into my ship, and bade my company follow me: so we came to the land of the Cyclops. Close to the shore was a cave, with laurels round about the mouth. This was the dwelling of the Cyclops. Alone he dwelt, a creature without law. Nor was he like to mortal men, but rather to some wooded peak of the hills that stands out apart from all the rest.

"Then I bade the rest of my comrades abide by the ship, and keep it, but I took twelve men, the bravest that there were in the crew, and went forth. I had with me a goat-skin full of the wine, dark red, and sweet, which the priest of Apollo [Footnote: A-pol'- lo.] at Ismarus had given me. So precious was it that none in his house knew of it saving himself and his wife. When they drank of it they mixed twenty measures of water with one of wine, and the smell that went up from it was wondrous sweet. No man could easily refrain from drinking it. With this wine I filled a great skin and bore it with me; also I bare corn in a pouch, for my heart within me told me that I should need it.

"So we entered the cave, and judged that it was the dwelling of some rich and skilful shepherd. For within there were pens for the young of the sheep and of the goats, divided all according to their age, and there were baskets full of cheeses, and full milkpails ranged along the wall. But the Cyclops himself was away in the pastures. Then my companions besought me that I would depart, taking with me, if I would, a store of cheeses and some of the lambs and of the kids. But I would not, for I wished to see what manner of host this strange shepherd might be, and, if it might be, to take a gift from his hand, such as is the due of strangers. Verily, his coming was not to be a joy to my company.

"It was evening when the Cyclops came home, a mighty giant, very tall of stature, and when we saw him we fled into the cave in great fear. On his shoulder he bore a vast bundle of pine logs for his fire, and threw them down outside the cave great crash, and drove the flocks within, and closed the entrance with a huge rock, which twenty wagons and more could not bear. Then he milked the ewes and all the she-goats, and half of the milk he curdled for cheese, and half he set ready for himself, when he should sup. Next he kindled a fire with the pine logs, and the flame lighted up all the cave, showing to him both me and my comrades.

"'Who are ye?' cried Polyphemus [Footnote: Pol-y-phe'-mus.], for that was the giant's name. 'Are ye traders or pirates?'

"I shuddered at the dreadful voice and shape, but bare me bravely, and answered: 'We are no pirates, mighty sir, but Greeks sailing back from Troy, and subjects of the great King Agamemnon, whose fame is spread from one end of heaven to the other. And we are come to beg hospitality of thee in the name of Zeus, who rewards or punishes hosts and guests according as they be faithful the one to the other, or no.'

"'Nay,' said the giant; 'it is but idle talk to tell me of Zeus and the other gods. We Cyclopes take no account of gods, holding ourselves to be much better and stronger than they. But come, tell me where have you left your ship?'

"But I saw his thought when he asked about the ship, for he was minded to break it, and take from us all hope of flight. Therefore I answered him craftily:—

"Ship have we none, for that which was ours King Poseidon brake, driving it on a jutting rock on this coast, and we whom thou seest are all that are escaped from the waves."

"Polyphemus answered nothing, but without more ado caught up two of the men, as a man might catch up the pups of a dog, and dashed them on the ground, and tare them limb from limb, and devoured them, with huge draughts of milk between, leaving not a morsel, not even the very bones. But we that were left, when we saw the dreadful deed, could only weep and pray to Zeus for help. And when the giant had filled his maw with human flesh and with the milk of the flocks, he lay down among his sheep and slept.

"Then I questioned much in my heart whether I should slay the monster as he slept, for I doubted not that my good sword would pierce to the giant's heart, mighty as he was. But my second thought kept me back, for I remembered that if I should slay him, I and my comrades would yet perish miserably. For who could move away the great rock that lay against the door of the cave? So we waited till the morning, with grief in our hearts. And the monster woke, and milked his flocks, and afterwards, seizing two men, devoured them for his meal. Then he went to the pastures, but put the great rock on the mouth of the cave, just as a man puts down the lid upon his quiver.

"All that day I was thinking what I might best do to save myself and my companions, and the end of my thinking was this. There was a mighty pole in the cave, green wood of an olive tree, big as a ship's mast, which Polyphemus purposed to use, when the smoke should have dried it, as a walking-staff. Of this I cut off a fathom's length, and my comrades sharpened it and hardened it in the fire, and then hid it away. At evening the giant came back, and drove his sheep into the cave, nor left the rams outside, as he had been wont to do before, but shut them in. And having duly done his shepherd's work, he took, as before, two of my comrades, and devoured them. And when he had finished his supper, I came forward, holding the wine-skin in my hand, and said:—

"'Drink, Cyclops, now that thou hast feasted. Drink, and see what precious things we had in our ship. But no one hereafter will come to thee with such, if thou dealest with strangers as cruelly as thou hast dealt with us.'

"Then the Cyclops drank, and was mightily pleased, and said: 'Give me again to drink, and tell me thy name, stranger, and I will give thee a gift such as a host should give. In good truth this is a rare liquor. We, too, have vines, but they bear not wine like this, which, indeed, must be such as the gods drink in heaven.'

"Then I gave him the cup again, and he drank. Thrice I gave it to him, and thrice he drank, not knowing what it was, and how it would work within his brain.

"Then I spake to him: 'Thou didst ask my name, Cyclops. My name is No Man. And now that thou knowest my name, thou shouldest give me thy gift.'

"And he said: 'My gift shall be that I will eat thee last of all thy company.'

"And as he spake, he fell back in a drunken sleep. Then I bade my comrades be of good courage, for the time was come when they should be delivered. And they thrust the stake of olive wood into the fire till it was ready, green as it was, to burst into flame, and they thrust it into the monster's eye; for he had but one eye and that was in the midst of his forehead, with the eyebrow below it. And I, standing above, leaned with all my force upon the stake, and turned it about, as a man bores the timber of a ship with a drill. And the burning wood hissed in the eye, just as the red-hot iron hisses in the water when a man seeks to temper steel for a sword.

"Then the giant leapt up, and tore away the stake, and cried aloud, so that all the Cyclopes who dwelt on the mountain-side heard him and came about his cave, asking him: 'What aileth thee, Polyphemus, that thou makest this uproar in the peaceful night, driving away sleep? Is any one robbing thee of thy sheep, or seeking to slay thee by craft or force?' And the giant answered, 'No Man slays me by craft.'

"'Nay, but,' they said, 'if no man does thee wrong, we cannot help thee. The sickness which great Zeus may send, who can avoid? Pray to our father, Poseidon, for help.'

"So they spake, and I laughed in my heart when I saw how I had deceived them by the name that I had given.

"But the Cyclops rolled away the great stone from the door of the cave, and sat in the midst, stretching out his hands, to feel whether perchance the men within the cave would seek to go out among the sheep.

"Long did I think how I and my comrades should best escape. At last I lighted upon a plan that seemed better than all the rest, and much I thanked Zeus because this once the giant had driven the rams with the other sheep into the cave. For, these being great and strong, I fastened my comrades under the bellies of the beasts, tying them with willow twigs, of which the giant made his bed. One ram I took, and fastened a man beneath it, and two others I set, one on either side. So I did with the six, for but six were left out of the twelve who had ventured with me from the ship. And there was one mighty ram, far larger than all the others, and to this I clung, grasping the fleece tight with both my hands. So we all waited for the morning. And when the morning came, the rams rushed forth to the pasture; but the giant sat in the door and felt the back of each as it went by, nor thought to try what might be underneath. Last of all went the great ram. And the Cyclops knew him as he passed, and said:—

"'How is this, thou who art the leader of the flock? Thou art not wont thus to lag behind. Thou hast always been the first to run to the pastures and streams in the morning, and the first to come back to the fold when evening fell; and now thou art last of all. Perhaps thou art troubled about thy master's eye, which some wretch—No Man, they call him—has destroyed. He has not escaped, and I would that thou couldest speak, and tell me where he is lurking. Of a truth, I would dash out his brains upon the ground, and avenge me on this No Man.'

"So speaking, he let the ram pass out of the cave. But when we were now out of reach of the giant, I loosed my hold of the ram, and then unbound my comrades. And we hastened to our ship, not forgetting to drive the sheep before us, and often looking back till we came to the seashore. Right glad were those that had abode by the ship to see us. Nor did they lament for those that had died, though we were fain to do so, for I forbade, fearing lest the noise of their weeping should betray where we were to the giant. Then we all climbed into the ship, and sitting well in order on the benches smote the sea with our oars, laying to right lustily, that we might the sooner get away from the accursed land. And when we had rowed a hundred yards or so, so that a man's voice could yet be heard by one who stood upon the shore, I stood up in the ship and shouted:—

"'He was no coward, O Cyclops, whose comrades thou didst so foully slay in thy den. Justly art thou punished, monster, that devourest thy guests in thy dwelling. May the gods make thee suffer yet worse things than these!'

"Then the Cyclops in his wrath brake off the top of a great hill, a mighty rock, and hurled it where he had heard the voice. Right in front of the ship's bow it fell, and a great wave rose as it sank, and washed the ship back to the shore. But I seized a long pole with both hands, and pushed the ship from the land, and bade my comrades ply their oars, nodding with my head, for I would not speak, lest the Cyclops should know where we were. Then they rowed with all their might and main.

"And when we had gotten twice as far as before, I made as if I would speak again; but my comrades sought to hinder me, saying: 'Nay, my lord, anger not the giant any more. Surely we thought before that we were lost, when he threw the great rock, and washed our ship back to the shore. And if he hear thee now, he may still crush our ship and us.'

"But I would not be persuaded, but stood up and said: 'Hear, Cyclops! If any man ask who blinded thee, say that it was the warrior Ulysses, son of Laertes, dwelling in Ithaca.'

"And the Cyclops answered with a groan: 'Of a truth, the old prophecies are fulfilled; for long ago there came to this land a prophet who foretold to me that Ulysses would rob me of my sight. But I looked for a great and strong man, who should subdue me by force, and now a weakling has done the deed, having cheated me with wine.'

"Then the Cyclops lifted up his hands to Poseidon and prayed: 'Hear me, Poseidon, if I am indeed thy son and thou my father. May this Ulysses never reach his home! or, if the Fates have ordered that he should reach it, may he come alone, all his comrades lost, and come to find sore trouble in his house!'

"And as he ended, he hurled another mighty rock, which almost lighted on the rudder's end, yet missed it as by a hair's breadth. And the wave that it raised was so great that it bare us to the other shore.

"So we came to the island of the wild goats, where we found our comrades, who, indeed, had waited long for us in sore fear lest we had perished. Then I divided amongst my company all the sheep which we had taken from the Cyclops. And all, with one consent, gave me for my share the great ram which had carried me out of the cave, and I sacrificed it to Zeus. And all that day we feasted right merrily on the flesh of sheep and on sweet wine, and when the night was come, we lay down upon the shore and slept.

CHAPTER XI
AEOLUS; THE LAESTRYGONS; CIRCE

(THE TALE OF ULYSSES)

"The next morning we set sail, and came, after a while, to the island where dwelleth AEolus. A floating island it is, and it hath about it an unbroken wall of bronze. For a whole month did the King entertain me in friendly fashion, and I told him the whole story of the things that had been done at Troy.

"Afterwards I told him of my journey, and asked help of him. And he gave me the skin of an ox nine years old, in which he had bound all the winds that were contrary to me, for Zeus hath made him keeper of the winds, that he may rouse them or put them to rest as he will. This pouch of ox-hide he bound fast to the deck of the ship with a thong of silver, that not a wind might escape from it. But he let a gentle west wind blow, that it might carry me and my comrades to our home. For nine days it blew, and now we were near to Ithaca, our country, so that we saw the men that tended the beacon-lights, for it was now near to the dawn on the tenth day.

"But now, by an ill chance, I fell asleep, being wholly wearied out, for I had held the helm for nine days, nor trusted it to any of my comrades. And while I slept my comrades, who had cast eyes of envy on the great ox-hide, said one to another:—

"'Strange it is how men love and honour this Ulysses whithersoever he goes. And now he comes back from Troy with much spoil, but we with empty hands. Let us see what it is that AEolus hath given him, for doubtless in this ox-hide is much silver and gold.'

"So they loosed the great bag of ox-hide, and lo! all the winds rushed out, and carried us far away from our country. And I, waking with the tumult, doubted much whether I should not throw myself into the sea and so die. But I endured, thinking it better to live. Only I veiled my face and so lay still while the ships drave before the winds, till we came again to the island of AEolus. Then we landed, and fetched water, and ate our meal by the side of our ships. And when our meal was ended, I took a herald and one of my company, and went to the palace of the King, and found him feasting with his wife and children, and I sat down on the threshold. Much did they wonder to see me, saying, 'What evil power has hindered thee, that thou didst not reach thy country and home?'

"Then I answered: 'Blame not me, but the evil counsels of my comrades, and sleep, which mastered me to my hurt. But do ye help me again.'

"But he said, 'Begone! we may not help him whom the gods hate; and hated of them thou surely art.'

"So AEolus sent me away. Then again we launched our ships and set forth, toiling wearily at the oars, and sad at heart.

"Six days we rowed, nor rested at night; and on the seventh we came to Lamos [Footnote: La'-mos.], which was a city of the Laestrygons, in whose land the night is as the day, so that a man might earn double wages, if only he wanted not sleep. There was a fair haven with cliffs about it, and a narrow mouth with great rocks on either side. And within are no waves.

"Now I made fast my ship to the rocks that were without, but the others entered the haven. Then I sent two men, and a herald with them, and these came upon a smooth road by which wagons brought down wood from the mountain to the city. Here they met a maiden, the daughter of the king of the land, and asked of her who was lord of that country. Thereupon she showed them her father's lofty palace. And they, entering this, saw the maiden's mother, big as a mountain, and horrible to behold, who straightway called to her husband. Then the messengers fled to the ships; but he made a great shout, and the giant Laestrygons came flocking about him. And these broke off great stones from the cliffs, each stone as much as a man could carry, and cast them at the ships, so that they were broken. And the men they speared, as if they were fishes, and devoured them. So it happened to all the ships in the haven. I only escaped, for I cut the hawser with my sword, and bade my men ply their oars, which indeed they did right willingly.

"After a while we came to the island where Circe dwelt, who is the daughter of the Sun. Two days and nights we lay upon the shore in great trouble and sorrow. On the third I took my spear and sword and climbed a hill, for I wished to see to what manner of land we had come. And having climbed it, I saw the smoke rising from the palace of Circe, where it stood in the midst of a wood. Then I thought awhile: should I go straightway to the palace that I saw, or first return to my comrades on the shore. And it seemed the better plan to go to the ship and bid my comrades make their midday meal, and afterwards send them to search out the place. But as I went, some god took pity on me, and sent a great stag, with mighty antlers, across my path. The stag was going down to the river to drink, for the sun was now hot; and casting my spear at it I pierced it through. Then I fastened together the feet with green withes and a fathom's length of rope, and slinging the beast round my neck, so carried it to the ship, leaning on my spear; for indeed it was heavy to bear, nor was it possible for me to carry it on my shoulder with one hand. And when I was come to the ship, I cast down my burden. Now the men were sitting with their faces muffled, so sad were they. But when I bade them be of good cheer, they looked up and marvelled at the great stag. And all that day we feasted on deer's flesh and sweet wine, and at night lay down to sleep on the shore. But when morning was come, I called my comrades together, and spake: 'I know not, friends, where we are. Only I know, having seen smoke yesterday from the hill, that there is a dwelling in this island.'

"It troubled the men much to hear this, for they thought of the Cyclops and of the Laestrygons; and they wailed aloud. Then I divided them into two companies. I set Eurylochus [Footnote: Eu- ryl'-o-chus.] over the one, and I myself took command of the other, and I shook lots in a helmet to see who should go and search out the island, and the lot of Eurylochus leapt out. So he went, and comrades twenty and two with him. And in an open space in the wood they found the palace of Circe. All about were wolves and lions; yet these harmed not the men, but stood up on their hind legs, fawning upon them, as dogs fawn upon their master when he comes from his meal, because he brings the fragments with him that they love. And the men were afraid. And they stood in the porch and heard the voice of Circe as she sang with a lovely voice and plied the loom. Then said Polites [Footnote: Po-li'-tes.], who was dearest of all my comrades to me, in whom also I most trusted: 'Some one within plies a great loom, and sings with a loud voice. Some goddess is she or a woman. Let us make haste and call.'

"So they called to her, and she came out and beckoned to them that they should follow. So they went, in their folly, all except Eurylochus. And she bade them sit, and mixed for them red wine and barley-meal and cheese and honey, and mighty drugs, of which, if a man drank, he forgot all that he loved. And when they had drunk, she smote them with her wand. And lo! they had of a sudden the heads and the voices and the bristles of swine, but the heart of a man was in them still. And Circe shut them in sties, and gave them acorns to eat.

"But Eurylochus fled back to the ship, bringing tidings of what had befallen his comrades. For a time he could not speak a word, so full was his heart of grief, and his eyes of tears. But, at last, when we had asked him many questions, he told us his tale.

"Thereupon I cast about my shoulder my silver-studded sword, and took my bow also, and bade him lead me by the way by which he had gone. But he caught me by both my hands, and besought me, saying: 'Take me not thither against my will; for I am persuaded that thou thyself wilt not return again, nor bring any of thy comrades. Let us that remain flee, and escape death.' Then I said, 'Stay here by the ship, eating and drinking, if it be thy will, but I must go.'

"And when I had come to the house, there met me Hermes of the golden wand, the messenger of the gods, in the shape of a fair youth, who said to me:—

"'Art thou come to rescue thy comrades that are now swine in Circe's house? Nay, but thou shalt never go back thyself. Yet stay; I will give thee a drug which shall give thee power to resist all her charms. For when she shall have mixed thee drink, and smitten thee with her wand, then do thou rush upon her with thy sword, as if thou wouldest slay her. And when she shall pray for peace, do thou make her swear by the great oath that binds the gods that she will not harm thee.'

"Then Hermes showed me a certain herb, whose root was black, but the flower white as milk. 'Moly,' the gods call it, and very hard it is for mortal man to find; but to the gods all things are possible.

"Thereupon Hermes departed to Olympus, but I went on to the palace of the goddess, much troubled in heart. When I came thither I stood in the porch and called, and Circe came, and opened the doors, and bade me come in.

"Then she set me on a great chair, skilfully carven, with a footstool for my feet. Afterward she gave me drink in a cup of gold, but she had mixed in it a deadly charm. This I drank, but was not bewitched, for the herb saved me. Then she smote me with her wand, saying: 'Go now to the sty and lie there with thy fellows.' Thereto upon I drew my sword, and rushed upon her, as though I would have slain her. Then she caught me by the knees, and cried aloud: 'Who art thou? What is thy race? I marvel that thou couldest drink of this drink that I have charmed, and yet take no hurt. I thought that there was no mortal man that could so do. Thou must have a soul against which there is no enchantment. Verily, thou must be that Ulysses who was to come to this island as he returned from Troy, for so Hermes told me. But come, let us be friends.' Then I said to her: 'Nay, goddess, but how can we two be friends, when thou hast turned my companions into swine. I fear thee that thou hast some deceit in thy heart, and thou wilt take me unawares, and do me a great mischief. But swear a mighty oath, even the oath by which the gods are bound, that thou wilt not harm me.'

"Then Circe sware the mighty oath, even the oath by which the gods are bound.

"After this her handmaids, who were fair women born of the springs and streams and woods, prepared a feast. One set coverlets of purple on the chairs, and another brought up tables of silver to the chair, and set on the tables baskets of gold. A third mixed sweet wine in a bowl of silver, and set thereby cups of gold; and the fourth filled a great kettle with water, and put fire under it. And when it boiled, she prepared a bath, and the bath took away the weariness from my limbs. And when I had bathed, a handmaid bare water in a pitcher of gold, and poured it over a basin of gold, that I might wash my hands. Then the housekeeper brought me wheaten bread, and set many dainties on the table; and Circe bade me eat; but I sat silent and sorrowful, having other thoughts in my mind.

"And when the goddess perceived that I was silent and ate not, she said: 'Why dost thou sit, Ulysses, as though thou wert dumb? Fearest thou any craft of mine? Nay, but that may not be, for have I not sworn the great oath that binds the gods?'

"Then I made answer, 'Nay, but who could think of meat and drink when such things had befallen his companions?'

"Then Circe led the way, holding her wand in her hand, and opened the doors of the sties, and drove out the swine that had been men. Then she rubbed on each another mighty drug, and the bristles fell from their bodies and they became men, only younger and fairer than before. And when they saw me, they clung to me and wept for joy, and Circe herself was moved with pity.

"Then said she to me: 'Go, Ulysses, to thy ship, and put away all the goods and tackling in the caves that are on the shore, but come again hither thyself, and bring thy comrades with thee.'

"Then I went. Right glad were they who had stayed to see me, glad as are the calves who have been penned in the fold-yard when their mothers come back in the evening.

"So we went to the dwelling of Circe, who feasted us royally, so that we remained with her for a whole year, well content.

"But when the year was out my companions said to me, 'It is well to remember thy country, if it is indeed the will of the gods that thou shouldest return thither.'

"Then I besought Circe that she would send me on my way homewards, as indeed she had promised to do. And she answered, saying:—

"'I would not have you abide in my house unwillingly. Yet must thou first go on another journey, even to the dwellings of the dead, there to speak with the seer [Footnote: seer, prophet] Teiresias [Footnote: Tei-re'-si-as].'

"But I was sore troubled to hear such things, and wept aloud, saying, 'Who shall guide us in this journey?—for never yet did ship make such a voyage as this.'

"Then Circe made answer: 'Son of Laertes, trouble not thyself because thou hast no guide, only set up the mast in thy ship, and spread out the sails, and sit thee down with thy companions, and the north wind shall carry thee to the place whereto thou art bound. When thou shalt have sailed across the stream of ocean, thou shalt come to a waste shore, where are many tall poplar trees and willows. Beach there thy ship on the shore of ocean, and go thyself to the dwelling of Hades.[Footnote: Ha'-des] There is a certain rock, and near to it meet two streams, the river of fire, and the river of wailing. Dig there a trench; it shall be a cubit [Footnote: cubit, a foot and a half] long and a, cubit broad; pour out therein a drink-offering to the dead; and sprinkle white barley thereon. And as thou doest these things, entreat the dead, and promise that when thou shalt come again to Ithaca, thou wilt offer a barren heifer, even the best thou hast, and that thou wilt sacrifice to Teiresias alone a black ram, the goodliest in the flock. And after thou hast made thy prayers to the dead, offer up a black ram and a black ewe. Then will come many spirits of the dead, but suffer them not to drink of the blood till thou shalt have spoken to Teiresias. Speedily will the seer come to thee, and will tell thee how thou mayest return to thy home.' The next morning I roused my companions, saying, 'Sleep no more; we will go on our way, for Circe hath shown to me the whole matter.'"So I spake, and they consented to my words. Yet did not I take all my company safe from the dwelling of the goddess. There was a certain Elpenor [Footnote: El-pe'-nor.], who was the youngest of them all, and was neither valiant nor of an understanding mind. He was sleeping apart from his fellows, on the housetop, for he had craved for the coolness of the air. He, hearing our voices, and the sound of the men's feet, as they moved hither and thither, leapt up of a sudden, and thought not to come down by the ladder by which he had gone up, but fell down from the roof, so that his neck was broken, and he went down to the dwellings of the dead.

"But as my men were on their way, I spake to them, saying: 'Ye think that ye are going to your native country; not so, for Circe hath showed me another journey that we must take, even to the dwelling of Hades, that I may speak with the spirit of Teiresias the seer.'"So I spake, and their spirit was broken within them, and they sat down where they were, and mourned, and tare their hair. But their weeping profited nothing.

"Meanwhile Circe had gone, and made fast a ram and a black ewe to the ship, passing on as we went, for none may mark the goings of the immortal gods."

CHAPTER XII
THE DWELLINGS OF THE DEAD

(THE TALE OF ULYSSES)

"After this we made ready the ship for sailing, and put the black sheep on board, and so departed; and Circe sent a wind from behind that filled the sails; and all the day through our ship passed quickly over the sea.

"And when the sun had set we came to the utmost border of the ocean. Then I bade two of my comrades make ready the sheep for sacrifice; and I myself dug a pit of a cubit every way, and poured in it a drink-offering of honey and milk, and sweet wine, and water, and sprinkled barley upon the drink-offering. Afterwards I took the sheep and slew them, so that their blood ran into the trench. And the dead were gathered to the place,— maidens, and old men who had borne the sorrows of many years, and warriors that had been slain in battle, having their arms covered with blood. All these gathered about the pit with a terrible cry; and I was sore afraid. Then I bade my comrades burn the carcasses of the sheep and pray to the gods of the dead; but I myself sat down by the pit's side, and would not suffer the souls of the dead to come near unto the blood until I had inquired of Teiresias.

"First of all came the soul of my comrade Elpenor. Much did I wonder to see him, and I asked, 'How comest thou hither, Elpenor, to the land of darkness? and how have thy feet outstripped my ship?' Then said Elpenor: 'I fell from the roof of the palace of Circe, not bethinking me of the ladder, and so brake my neck. But now, I pray thee, if thou lovest wife and father and son, forget me not, when thou returnest to the island of Circe. Burn me with fire and my arms with me; and make a mound for me by the shore of the sea, that men may hear of me and of my fate in after time. And set up my oar upon my tomb, even the oar which I was wont to ply among my comrades.'

"Then I said to him, 'All this shall be done as thou desirest.'

"And we sat on either side of the trench as we talked, and I held my sword over the blood.

"After him came to me the soul of my mother, whom I had left alive when I sailed to Troy. Sorely I wept to see her, yet suffered her not to come near and drink of the blood till I had inquired of Teiresias. Then came Teiresias, holding a golden sceptre in his hand, and spake, saying: 'Why hast thou left the light of day, and come hither to this land of the dead, wherein is no delight? But come, depart from the pit, and take away thy sword, that I may come near and tell thee true.'

"So I thrust my sword into the scabbard; and Teiresias drank of the blood; and when he had drunk, he spake: 'Thou seekest to hear of thy going back to thy home. Know, therefore, that it shall be with peril and toil. For Poseidon will not easily lay aside his wrath against thee, because thou didst take from his dear son, the Cyclops, the sight of his eye. Yet for all this ye may yet come safe to your home, if only thou canst restrain thyself and thy comrades when ye come to the island of the Three Capes, and find there the oxen and the sheep of the Sun. If ye let them be and harm them not, then may ye yet return to Ithaca, though after dreadful toil. But if not, then shall ye perish. And if thou escape thyself, after long time shalt thou return, having lost all thy comrades, and the ship of strangers shall carry thee; and thou shalt find trouble in thy house, men of violence who devour thy substance while they seek thy wife in marriage.'

"To him I made answer: 'So be it, Teiresias. All these things the gods have ordered after their own will. But tell me this. Here I see the soul of my mother that is dead; and she sits near the blood, but regards me not, nor speaks to me. How can she know that I am indeed her son?'

"Then said Teiresias: 'Whomsoever of the dead thou shalt suffer to drink of the blood, he will speak to thee; but whomsoever thou sufferest not, he will depart in silence.'

"So I abode in my place; and the soul of my mother came near and drank of the blood. And when she had drunk, she knew her son, and said: 'My son, why hast thou come into the land of darkness, being yet alive? Hast thou not yet returned to thy home?'

"To her I made answer: 'I came hither to inquire of Teiresias of Thebes, and my home have I not seen. Truly trouble hath followed me from the day that I first went with King Agamemnon to the land of Troy. But tell me, how didst thou die? Did a wasting disease slay thee, or did Artemis [Footnote: Ar'-te-mis] smite thee with a sudden stroke of her arrow? And my father and my son, have they enjoyment of that which is mine, or have others taken it from them? And my wife, is she true to me, or hath she wedded some prince among the Greeks?'

"Then said my mother: 'Thy wife is true, and sits weeping for thee day and night. And thy son hath enjoyment of thy possessions, and hath his due place at the feasts of the people. But thy father cometh no longer to the city, but abideth in the country. Nor hath he any couch for his bed, but in winter-time he sleeps, even as sleep the slaves, in the ashes near unto the fire, and when the summer comes, in the corner of the vineyard upon leaves. Greatly doth he sorrow, waiting for thy return, and the burden of old age lies heavy upon him. But as for me, no wasting disease slew me, nor did Artemis smite me with her arrows; but I died of longing for thee, so sorely did I miss thy wisdom and thy love.'

"Then I was fain to lay hold upon the soul of my mother. Thrice I sprang forward, eager to embrace her, and thrice she passed from out my hands, even as passeth a shadow. And when I said, 'How is this, my mother? art thou then but a phantom that the queen of the dead hath sent me?' my mother answered me: 'Thus it is with the dead, my son. They have no more any flesh and bones; for these the fire devours; but their souls are even as dreams, flying hither and thither. But do thou return so soon as may be to the light, and tell all that thou hast seen and heard to thy wife.'

"Thereupon I departed from the place, and bade my comrades embark upon the ships and loose the ropes. And we embarked and sat upon the benches; and the great stream of Ocean bare us onward, rowing at the first, and afterwards hoisting the sails."

CHAPTER XIII
THE SIRENS; SCYLLA; THE OXEN OF THE SUN

(THE TALE OF ULYSSES)

"It was now evening when we came back to the island of Circe. Therefore we beached the ship, and lay down by the sea, and slept till the morning. And when it was morning we arose, and went to the palace of Circe, and fetched thence the body of our comrade Elpenor. We raised the funeral pile where the farthest headland runs out into the sea, and burned the dead man and his arms; then we raised a mound over his bones, and put a pillar on the top of the mound, and on the top of the pillar his oar.

"But Circe knew of our coming, and of what we had done, and she came and stood in our midst, her handmaids coming with her, and bearing flesh and bread and wine in plenty. Then she spake, saying: 'Overbold are ye, who have gone down twice into the house of death which most men see but once. Come now, eat and drink this day; to-morrow shall ye sail again over the sea, and I will tell you the way, and declare all that shall happen, that ye may suffer no hindrance as ye go.'

"So all that day we ate and feasted. And when the darkness came over the land, my comrades lay them down by the ship and slept. But Circe took me by the hand, and led me apart from my company, and inquired of what I had seen and done. And when I had told her all my tale, she spake, saying: 'Hearken now to what I shall tell thee. First of all thou shalt come to the Sirens, who bewitch all men with their singing. For whoever cometh nigh to them, and listeneth to their song, he seeth not wife or children any more; for the Sirens enchant him, and draw him to where they sit, with a great heap of dead men's bones about them. Speed thy ship past them, and first fill the ears of thy comrades with wax, lest any should hear the song; but if thou art minded thyself to hear the song, let them bind thee fast to the mast. So shalt thou hear the song, and take no harm. And if thou shalt entreat thy comrades to loose thee, they must bind the bonds all the faster.

"'When thou shalt have passed the island of the Sirens, then thou must choose for thyself which path thou shalt take. On the one side are the rocks that men call the Wandering Rocks. By these not even winged creatures can pass unharmed. No ship can pass them by unhurt; all round them do the waves toss timbers of broken ships and bodies of men that are drowned. One ship only hath ever passed them by, even the ship Argo, and even her would the waves have dashed upon the rocks, but that Hera [Footnote: He'-ra], for love of Jason [Footnote: Ja'-son], caused her to pass by.

"'These there are on the one side, and on the other are two rocks. The first rock reacheth with a sharp peak to the heavens, and about the peak is a dark cloud that passeth not away from it, no, not in summer time or harvest. This rock no man could climb, even though he had twenty hands and feet, for it is steep and smooth. In the midst of this cliff is a cave wherein dwelleth Scylla, the dreadful monster of the sea. Her voice is but as the voice of a new-born dog, and her twelve feet are small and ill-grown, but she hath six necks, exceeding long, and on each a head dreadful to behold, and in each head three rows of teeth, thick set and full of death. She is hidden up to her middle in the cave, but she putteth her heads out of it, fishing for dolphins, or sea-dogs, or other creatures of the sea, for indeed there are countless flocks of them. No ship can pass her by unharmed, for with each head she carrieth off a man, snatching them from the ship's deck. Hard by, even a bow-shot off, is the other rock, lower by far, and with a great fig tree growing on the top. Beneath it Charybdis [Footnote: Cha-ryb'-dis] thrice a day sucketh in the water, and thrice a day spouteth it forth. If thou chance to be there when she sucks it in, not even Poseidon's help could save thee. See, therefore, that thou guide thy ship near to Scylla rather than to the other, for it is better 'for thee to lose six men out of thy ship than all thy company together.'

"So Circe spake, and I said: 'Tell me, goddess, can I by any means escape from Charybdis on the one hand, and. on the other, avenge me on this monster, when she would take my comrades for a prey?'

"But the goddess said: 'Overbold thou art, and thinkest ever of deeds of battle. Verily, thou wouldest do battle with the gods themselves; and surely Scylla is not of mortal race, and against her there is no help. Thou wilt do better to flee. For if thou tarry to put on thy armour, then will she dart forth again, and take as many as before. Drive on thy ship, therefore, with what speed may be.

"'After this, thou wilt come to the island of the Three Capes, where are the herds and the flocks of the Sun. Seven herds of kine there are and seven flocks of sheep, and fifty in each. These neither are born, nor die, and they have two goddesses to herd them. If ye do these no hurt, then shall ye return, all of you, to Ithaca, but if ye harm them, then shall thy ship be broken, and all thy company shall perish, and thou shalt return alone and after long delay.'

"Having so spoken, the goddess departed. Then I roused my men and they launched the ship, and smote the water with their oars, and the goddess sending a favourable wind, we hoisted the sails, and rested.

"But, as we went, I spake to my companions, saying: 'Friends, it is not well that one or two only should know the things that Circe prophesied to me.

Therefore I will declare them to you, that we may know beforehand the things that shall come to pass, and so either die or live.'

"And first I told them of the Sirens; and while I spake we came to the Sirens' Island. Then did the breeze cease, and there was a windless calm. So my comrades took down the sails and put out the oars, and I cleft a great round of wax with my sword, and, melting it in the sun, I filled the ears of my men; afterwards they bound me by hands and feet, as I stood upright by the mast. And when we were so near the shore that the shout of a man could be heard therefrom, the Sirens perceived the ship, and began their song. And their song was this:—

"'Hither, come hither, renowned Odysseus, great glory of the Greeks. Here stay thy bark that thou mayest listen to the voice of us twain. For none hath ever driven by this way in his black ship, till he hath heard from our lips the voice sweet as the honeycomb, and hath had joy thereof and gone on his way the wiser. For lo, we know all things, all that the Greeks and the Trojans have suffered in wide Troy-land, yea, and we know all that shall hereafter be upon the fruitful earth.'

"Then I motioned my men to loose me, for their ears were stopped; but they plied their oars, and Eurylochus put new bonds upon me. And when we had passed by the island, then they took the wax from their ears, and loosed my bonds.

"After this they saw a smoke and surf, and heard a mighty roar, and their oars dropped out of their hands for fear; but I bade them be of good heart, because by my counsel they had escaped other dangers in past time. And the rowers I bade row as hard as they might. But to the helmsman I said: 'Steer the ship outside the smoke and the surf, and steer close to the cliffs.' But of Scylla I said nothing, fearing lest they should lose heart, and cease rowing altogether. Then I armed myself, and stood in the prow waiting till Scylla should appear.

"So we sailed up the strait; and there was sore trouble in my heart, for on the one side was Scylla, and on the other Charybdis, sucking down the water in a terrible fashion. Now would she vomit it forth, boiling the while as a great kettle boils upon the fire, and the spray fell on the very tops of the cliffs on either side. And then again she gulped the water down, so that we could see to her very depths, even the white sand that was at the bottom of the sea. Towards her we looked, fearing destruction, and while we looked, Scylla caught out of my ship six of my companions, the strongest and bravest of them all. When I looked to my ships to find my crew, then I saw their feet and hands, and I heard them call me by name, speaking to me for the last time. Even as a fisher, standing on some headland, lets down his long line with a bait, that he may ensnare the fishes of the sea, and each, as he catches it, he flings writhing ashore, so did Scylla bear the men writhing up the cliff to her cave. There did she devour them; and they cried to me terribly the while. Verily, of all the things that I have seen upon the sea, this was the most piteous of all.

"After this we came to the island of the Three Capes; and from my ship I heard the lowing of the kine and the bleating of the sheep. Thereupon I called to mind the saying of Teiresias, how he charged me to shun the island of the Sun. So I spake to my comrades, saying: 'Hear now the counsels of Teiresias and Circe. They charged me to sail by the island of the Sun; for they said that there the most dreadful evil would overtake us. Do ye then row the ship past.'

"So I spake; but Eurylochus made answer in wrath: 'Surely, Ulysses, thou knowest not weariness, and art made of iron, forbidding us, weary though we be with toil and watching, to land upon this island, where we might well refresh ourselves. Rash, also, art thou in that thou commandest us to sail all night; at night deadly winds spring up, and how shall we escape, if some sudden storm from the west or the south smite our ship, and break it in pieces? Rather let us stay, and take our meal and sleep by the ship's side, and to-morrow will we sail again across the sea.'

"Thus he spake, and all consented to his speech. Then I knew that the gods were minded to work us mischief, and I made answer: 'Ye force me, being many against one. But swear ye all an oath, that if ye find here either herd or flock, ye will not slay either bullock or sheep, but will rest content with the food that Circe gave us.'

"Then they all made oath that they would so do; and when they had sworn, they moored the ship within a creek, where there was a spring of fresh water; and so we took our meal. But when we had enough of meat and drink, we remembered our comrades whom Scylla had snatched from the ship and devoured and we mourned for them till slumber fell upon us.

"The next morning I spake to my company, saying: 'Friends, we have yet food, both bread and wine. Keep, therefore, your hands from the flocks and herds, lest some mischief overtake us, for they are the flocks and herds of the Sun, a mighty god whose eye none may escape.'

"With these words I persuaded them. But for a month the south wind blew without ceasing; there was no other wind, unless it were haply the east. So long, indeed, as the bread and wine failed not the men, they harmed not the herds, fearing to die. And afterwards, when our stores were consumed, they wandered about the island, and searched for food, snaring fishes and birds with hooks, for hunger pressed them sorely. But I roamed by myself, praying to the gods that they would send us deliverance. So it chanced one day that slumber overcame me, and I slept far away from my companions.

"Meanwhile Eurylochus spake to the others, using fatal craft: 'Friends, listen to one who suffers affliction with you. Always is death a thing to be avoided; but of all deaths the most to be feared is death by hunger. Come, therefore, let us sacrifice to the gods in heaven the best of the oxen of the Sun. And we will vow to build to the Sun, when we shall reach the land of Ithaca, a great temple which we will adorn with gifts many and precious. But if he be minded to sink our ship, being wroth for his oxen's sake, verily I would rather drown than waste slowly to death upon this island.'

"To this they all gave consent. Then Eurylochus drave the fattest of the kine,—for they grazed near the ship,—and the men sacrificed it to the gods.

"And one of the nymphs that herded the kine flew to the Sun with tidings of that which had been done. Then spake the Sun among the other gods: 'Avenge me now on the guilty comrades of Ulysses; for they have slain the herds which I delight to see both when I mount the heavens and when I descend therefrom. Verily, if they pay not the due penalty for their wrong-doing, I will go down and give my light to the regions of the dead.'

"Then Zeus made answer: 'Shine, thou Sun, as aforetime, on the earth. Verily, my thunderbolt can easily reach the bark of these sinners, and break it in the middle of the sea.'

"All these things I heard afterwards from the nymph Calypso, and she had heard them from Hermes, the messenger.

"With angry words did I rebuke my comrades, but found no remedy for their wrong-doing, seeing that the kine were dead. For six days my friends feasted on the cattle of the Sun; but when the seventh day came, we launched our ship upon the sea, and set sail.

"When we were now out of sight of the island of the Three Capes, and no other land appeared, Zeus hung a dark cloud over us, and suddenly the west wind came fiercely down upon the ship, and snapped the shrouds on either side. Thereupon the mast fell backward and brake the skull of a pilot, so that he plunged, as a diver plunges, into the sea. Meantime Zeus hurled his thunderbolt into the ship, filling it with sulphur from end to end. Then my comrades fell from the ship; I saw them carried about it like sea-gulls. But I still abode on the ship, till the sides were parted from the keel; then I bound myself with a leathern thong to the mast and the keel—for these were fastened together. On these I sat, being driven by the wind. All night long was I driven; and with the morning I came again to Scylla and to Charybdis. It was the time when she sucked in the waves; but I, borne upward by a wave, took fast hold of the branches of the wild fig tree that grew upon the rock. To this I clung for a long time, but knew not how to climb higher up. So I watched till she should vomit forth again the keel and the mast, for these she had swallowed up. And when I saw them again, then I plunged down from the rock, and caught hold of them, and seated myself on them; I rowed hard with the palms of my hands; and the father of the gods suffered not Scylla to espy me, or I should surely have perished. For nine days I floated, and on the tenth the gods carried me to the island of Calypso."

CHAPTER XIV
ITHACA

When Ulysses had ended his tale there was silence for a space throughout the hall. And after a while King Alcinous spake, saying: "Ulysses, now thou art come to my house, thou shalt no longer be kept from thy return. And on you, chiefs of the Phaeacians, I lay this command. Garments and gold are already stored for this stranger in a chest. Let us now, also, give him each a gift."

This saying pleased the princes, and they went each man to his house; and the next day they brought the gifts; and the King himself bestowed them under the benches, that the rowers might not be hindered in their rowing.

When these things were finished, the princes betook them to the palace of the King; and he sacrificed an ox to Zeus, and they feasted, and the minstrel sang. But still Ulysses would ever look to the sun, as if he would have hastened his going down; for indeed he was very desirous to return as a man desireth his supper, when he hath been driving the plough all day through a field with a yoke of oxen before him, and is right glad when the sun sinketh in the west, so Ulysses was glad at the passing of the daylight. And he spake, saying:—

"Pour out, now, the drink-offering, my lord the King, and send me on my way. Now do I bid you farewell, for ye have given me all that my heart desired, noble gifts and escort to my home. May the gods give me with them good luck, and grant, also, that I may find my wife and my friends in my home unharmed! And may ye abide here in joy with your wives and children, and may ye have all manner of good things and may no evil come near you."

Then spake the King to his squire: "Mix, now, the bowl, and serve out the wine, that we may pray to Zeus, and send the stranger on his way."

So the squire mixed the wine, and served it out; and they all made offering, and prayed.

Then Ulysses rose in his place, and placed the cup in the hand of Arete, the Queen, and spake: "Fare thee well, O Queen, till old age and death, which no man may escape, shall come upon thee! I go to my home; and do thou rejoice in thy children and in thy people, and in thy husband, the King."

When he had so said, he stepped over the threshold. And Alcinous sent with him a squire to guide him to the ship, and Arete sent maidens, bearing fresh clothing, and bread and wine. When they came to the ship, the rowers took the things, and laid them in the hold. Also they spread for Ulysses a rug and a linen sheet in the hinder part of the ship, that his sleep might be sound.

When these things were ended Ulysses climbed on board, and lay down; and the men sat upon the benches, and unbound the hawser. And it came to pass that so soon as they touched the water with the oars, a deep sleep fell upon him. As four horses carry a chariot quickly over the plain, so quick did the ship pass over the waves Not even a hawk, that is the swiftest of all flying things, could have kept pace with it.

And when the star that is the herald of the morning came up in the heaven, then did the ship approach the island. There is a certain harbour in Ithaca, the harbour of Phorcys [Footnote: Phor'-cys], the sea-god, where two great cliffs on either side break the force of the waves; a ship that can win her way into it can ride safely without moorings. And at the head of this harbour there is an olive tree, and a cave hard by which is sacred to the nymphs. Two gates hath the cave, one looking towards the north, by which men may enter, and one towards the south, which belongeth only to the gods. To this place the Phaeacians guided the ship, for they knew it well. Half the length of the keel did they run her ashore, so quickly did they row her. Then they lifted Ulysses out of the stern as he lay in the sheet and the rug which the Queen had given him. And still he slept. They took out also the gifts which the princes of the Phaeacians had given him, and laid them in a heap by the trunk of the olive tree, a little way from the road, lest some passer-by should rob him while he slept. After this they departed homeward.

But Poseidon still remembered his anger, and said to Zeus: "Now shall I be held in dishonour among the gods, for mortal men, even these Phaeacians, who are of my own kindred, pay me no regard. I said that this Ulysses should return in great affliction to his home; and now they have carried him safely across the sea, with such a store of gifts as he never would have won out of Troy, even had he come back unharmed with all his share of the spoil."

To him Zeus made answer: "What is that thou sayest, lord of the sea? How can the gods dishonour thee, who art the eldest among them? And if men withhold from thee the worship that is due, thou canst punish them after thy pleasure. Do, therefore, as thou wilt."

Then said Poseidon: "I would have done so long since, had not I feared thy wrath. But now I will smite this ship of the Phaeacians as she cometh back from carrying this man to his home. So shall they learn henceforth not to send men homeward; and their city will I overshadow with a great mountain."

And Zeus made answer to him, "Do as thou wilt."

Then Poseidon came down to the land of the Phaeacians, and there he tarried till the ship came near, speeding swiftly on her way. Thereupon he struck her, changing her into a stone, and rooting her to the bottom of the sea.

But the Phaeacians said one to another: "Who is this that hath hindered our ship, as she journeyed homeward? Even now she was plain to see."

But King Alcinous spake, saying: "Now are the prophecies fulfilled which my father was wont to speak. For he said that Poseidon was wroth with us because we carried men safely across the sea, and that one day the god would smite one of our ships, and change it into a stone, and that he would also overshadow our city with a great mountain. Now, therefore, let us cease from conveying men to their homes, and let us do sacrifice to Poseidon, slaying twelve bulls, that he overshadow not our city with a great mountain."

So the King spake, and the princes did as he commanded them.

Meanwhile Ulysses awoke in the land of Ithaca, and he knew not the place, for Athene had spread a great mist about it, doing it, as will be seen, with a good purpose, that he might safely accomplish that which it was in his heart to do. Then Ulysses started up, and made lament, saying: "Woe is me! To what land am I come? Are the men barbarous and unjust, or are they hospitable and righteous? Whither shall I carry these riches of mine? And whither shall I go myself? Surely the Phaeacians have dealt unfairly with me, for they promised that they would carry me back to my own country, but now they have taken me to a strange land. May Zeus punish them therefor! But let me first see to my goods, and reckon them up, lest the men should have taken some of them."

Thereupon he numbered the treasure and found that nothing was wanting. But not the less did he bewail him for his country.

But as he walked, lamenting, by the shore, Athene met him, having the likeness of a young shepherd, fair to look upon, such as are the sons of kings. Ulysses was glad when he saw her, though he knew her not, and said: "Friend, thou art the first man that I have seen in this land. Now, therefore, I pray thee to save my substance, and myself also. But first, tell me true— what land is this to which I am come, and what is the people? Is it an island, or a portion of the mainland?"

And the false shepherd said: "Thou art foolish, or, may be, hast come from very far, not to know this country. Many men know it, both in the east and in the west. Rocky it is, not fit for horses, nor is it very broad; but it is fertile land, and good for wine; nor does it want for rain, and a good pasture it is for oxen and goats; and men call it Ithaca. Even in Troy, which is very far, they say, from this land of Greece, men have heard of Ithaca."

This Ulysses was right glad to hear. Yet he was not minded to say who he was, but rather to feign a tale.

So he said: "Yes, of a truth, I heard of this Ithaca in Crete, from which I am newly come, with all this wealth, leaving also as much behind for my children. For I slew the son of the King, because he would have taken from me my spoil. And certain Phoenicians [Footnote: Phoe-ni'-ci-ans] agreed to take me to Pylos or to Elis;[Footnote: E'-lis] but the wind drave them hither, and while I slept they put me upon the shore, and my possessions with me, and departed."

This pleased Athene much, and she changed her shape, becoming like to a woman, tall and fair, and said to Ulysses:—

"Right cunning would he be who could cheat thee. Even now in thy native country thou dost not cease thy cunning words and deceits! But let these things be; for thou art the wisest of mortal men, and I excel among the gods in counsel. For I am Athene, daughter of Zeus, who am ever wont to stand by thee and help thee. And now we will hide these possessions of thine; and thou must be silent, nor tell to any one who thou art, and endure many things, so that thou mayest come to thine own again,"

To her Ulysses made answer: "It is hard for a mortal man to know thee, O goddess, however wise he may be, for thou takest many shapes. While I was making war against Troy with the other Greeks, thou wast ever kindly to me. But from the time that we took the city of Priam, and set sail for our homes, I saw thee not, until thou didst meet me in the land of the Phaeacians, comforting me, and guiding me thyself into the city. And now I beseech thee, by thy Father Zeus, to tell me truly: is this Ithaca that I see, for it seems to me that I have come to some other country, and that thou dost mock me. Tell me, therefore, whether in very deed I am come to mine own country."

Then Athene answered him: "Never will I leave thee, for indeed thou art wise and prudent above all others. For any other man, so coming back after many wanderings, would have hastened to see his wife and his children; but thou will first make trial of thy wife. Come now, I wilt show thee this land of Ithaca, that thou mayest be assured in thy heart. Lo! here is the harbour of Phorcys; here at the harbour's head is the olive tree; here also is the pleasant cave that is sacred to the nymphs, and there, behold, is the wooded hill."

Then the goddess scattered the mist, so that he saw the land. Then, indeed, he knew it for Ithaca, and he kneeled down and kissed the ground, and prayed to the nymphs, saying: "Never did I think to see you again; but now I greet you lovingly. Many gifts also will I give you, if Athene be minded, of her grace, to bring me to my own again." Then said Athene: "Take heart, and be not troubled. But first let us put away thy goods safely in the secret place of the cave."

Then Ulysses brought up the brass, and the gold, and the raiment that the Phaeacians had given him, and they two stored it in the cave, and Athene laid a great stone upon the mouth.

And Athene said: "Think, man of many devices, how thou wilt lay hands on these men, suitors of thy wife, who for three years have sat in thy house devouring thy substance. And she hath answered them craftily, making many promises, but still waiting for thy coming."

Then Ulysses said: "Truly I should have perished but for thee. But do thou help me, as of old in Troy, for with thee at my side I would fight with three hundred men."

Then said Athene: "Lo! I will cause that no man shall know thee, for I will wither the fair flesh on thy limbs, and take the bright hair from thy head, and make thine eyes dull. And the suitors shall take no account of thee, neither shall thy wife nor thy son know thee. But go to the swineherd Eumaeus [Footnote: Eu-mae'- us.], where he dwells by the fountain of Arethusa [Footnote: A-re- thu'-sa.], for he is faithful to thee and to thy house. And I will hasten to Sparta, to the house of Menelaus, to fetch Telemachus, for he went thither, seeking news of thee."

But Ulysses said to the goddess: "Why didst thou not tell him, seeing that thou knewest all? Was it that he too might wander over the seas in great affliction, and that others meanwhile might consume his goods?"

Then Athene made reply: "Trouble not thyself concerning him. I guided him myself that he might earn a good report, as a son searching for his father. Now he sitteth in peace in the hall of Menelaus. And though there are some that lie in wait for him to slay him, yet shall they not have their will. Rather shall they perish themselves and others with them that have devoured thy goods."

Then she touched him with her rod. She caused his skin to wither, and wasted the hair upon his head, and made his skin as the skin of an old man, and dimmed his eyes. His garments she changed so that they became torn and filthy and defiled with smoke. Over all she cast the skin of a great stag from which the hair was worn. A staff also she gave him, and a tattered pouch, and a rope wherewith to fasten it.

CHAPTER XV
EUMAEUS, THE SWINEHERD

Athene departed to Lacedaemon that she might fetch Telemachus, and Ulysses went to the house of Eumaeus, the swineherd. A great courtyard there was, and twelve sties for the sows, and four watch-dogs, fierce as wild beasts. In each sty were penned fifty swine; but the hogs were fewer in number, for the suitors ever devoured them at their feasts. There were but three hundred and threescore in all. The swineherd himself was shaping sandals, and of his men three were with the swine in the fields, and one was driving a fat beast to the city, to be meat for the suitors. But when Ulysses came near, the dogs ran upon him, and he dropped his staff and sat down, and yet would have suffered harm, even on his own threshold; but the swineherd ran forth and drave them away with stones, and spake unto his lord, though, indeed, he knew him not, saying:—

"Old man, the dogs came near to killing thee. That would, indeed, have been a shame and a grief to me; and, verily, I have other griefs in plenty. Here I sit and sorrow for my lord, and rear the fat swine for others to devour, while he, perchance, wanders hungry over the deep, or in the land of strangers, if, indeed, he lives. But come now, old man, to my house, and tell me who thou art, and what sorrows thou hast thyself endured."

Then the swineherd led him to his dwelling, and set him down on a seat of brushwood, with the hide of a wild goat spread on it. The hide was both large and soft, and he was wont himself to sleep on it.

Greatly did Ulysses rejoice at this welcome, and he said, "Now may Zeus and the other gods grant thee thy heart's desire, with such kindness hast thou received me!"

The swineherd made answer: "It were a wicked thing in me to slight a stranger, for the stranger and the beggar are from Zeus. But from us that are thralls and in fear of our master, even a little gift is precious. And the gods have stayed the return of my master. Had he come back he would surely have given me a house, and a portion of land, and a fair wife withal; for such things do lords give to servants that serve them well. Well would my lord have rewarded me, had he tarried at home. But now he hath perished. For he, too, went to Troy, that Agamemnon and Menalaus, his brother, might take vengeance on the Trojans."

Then he went away to the sties, and brought from thence two young pigs, and singed them, and cut them into pieces, and broiled them upon spits.

And when he had cooked them, he set them before the beggar man. He also mixed wine in a bowl of ivy-wood, and sat down opposite his guest, and bade him eat, saying: "Eat now such food as I can give thee; as for the fat hogs, them the suitors devour. Truly these men have no pity, nor fear of the gods. They must have heard that my lord is dead, so wickedly do they behave themselves. They do not woo as other suitors woo, nor do they go back to their own houses, but they sit at ease, and devour our wealth without stint. Once my lord had possessions beyond all counting; none in Ithaca nor on the mainland had so much. Hear now the sum of them: on the mainland twenty herds of kine, and flocks of sheep as many, and droves of swine as many, and as many herds of goats. Also here at this island's end he had eleven flocks of goats. Day by day do they take one of the goats for the suitors, and I take for them the best of the hogs."

So he spake, and Ulysses ate flesh and drank wine the while; but not a word did he speak, for he was planning the suitors' death. But at the last he spake: "My friend, who was this, thy lord, of whom thou speakest? Thou sayest that he perished, seeking to get vengeance for King Menelaus. Tell me now, for it may be that I have seen him, for I have wandered far."

But Eumaeus said: "Nay, old man, thus do all wayfarers talk, yet we hear no truth from them. Not a vagabond fellow comes to this island but our Queen must see him, and ask him many things, weeping the while. And thou, I doubt not, would tell a wondrous tale. But Ulysses, I know, is dead, and either the fowls of the air devour him, or the fishes of the sea."

But the false beggar said: "Hearken now, I swear to thee that Ulysses will return. And so soon as this shall come to pass thou shalt let me have the reward of good tidings. A mantle and a tunic shalt thou give me. But before it shall happen, I will take nothing, though my need be sore. Now Zeus be my witness, and this hospitable hearth of Ulysses to which I am come, that all these things shall come to pass even as I have said. This year shall Ulysses return; yea, while the moon waneth he shall come, and take vengeance on all who dishonour his name."

But Eumaeus made answer: "It is not I, old man, that shall ever pay the reward of good tidings. Truly, Ulysses will never more come back to his home. But let us turn our thought to other things. Bring thou not these to my remembrance any more; for, indeed, my heart is filled with sorrow, if any man put me in mind of my lord. As for thine oath, let it be. Earnestly do I pray that Ulysses may indeed return; for this is my desire, and the desire of his wife, and of the old man Laertes, and of Telemachus. And now I am troubled concerning Telemachus also. I thought that he would be no worse a man than his father; but some one, whether it were god or man I know not, took away his wits, and he went to Pylos, seeking news of his father. And now the suitors lie in wait for him, desiring that the race of Ulysses may perish utterly out of the land. Come now, old man, and tell me who art thou, and whence? On what ship did thou come, for that by ship thou earnest to Ithaca I do not doubt."

Then Ulysses answered: "Had we food and wine to last us for a year, and could sit quietly here and talk, while others go to their work, so long I should be in telling thee fully all my troubles that I have endured upon the earth."

Then he told a false tale,—how he was a Cretan who had been shipwrecked, and after many sufferings had reached Thesprotia [Footnote: Thes-pro'ti-a.], where he had heard of Ulysses. And when he sailed thence, the sailors were minded to sell him as a slave, but he had broken his bonds, and swam ashore, when they were near the island, and had hidden himself in the woods.

Then said the swineherd: "Stranger, thou hast stirred my heart with the tale of all that thou hast suffered. But in this thing, I fear, thou speakest not aright, saying that Ulysses will return. Well I know that he was hated of the gods, because they smote him not when he was warring against the men of Troy, nor afterwards among his friends, when the war was ended. Then would the host have built for him a great mound; and he would have won great renown for himself and for his children. But now he hath perished ingloriously by the storms of the sea. As for me, I dwell apart with the swine, and go not into the city, save when there have been brought, no man knows whence, some tidings of my master. Then all the people sit about the bringer of news, and question him, both those who desire their lord's return, and those who delight in devouring his substance without recompense. But I care not to ask questions, since the time when a certain AEtolian [Footnote: AE-to'-li-an.] cheated me with his story. He too had slain a man, and had wandered over many lands, and when he came to my house, I dealt kindly with him. This fellow said that he had seen my lord with the King of Crete, and that he was mending his ships which the storm had broken. Also he said that he would come home when it was summer, or harvest time, and would bring much wealth with him. But thou, old man, seek not to gain my favour with lies, nor to comfort me with idle words."

But Ulysses answered: "Verily, thou art slow of heart to believe. Even with an oath have I not persuaded thee. But come, let us make an agreement together, and the gods shall be our witnesses. If thy lord shall return, then shalt thou give me a mantle and a tunic, and send me on my way, whither I desire to go. But if he come not back according to my word, then let thy men throw me down from a great rock, that others may fear to deceive."

Then the swineherd said: "Much credit, truly, should I gain among men, if, having entertained thee in my house, I should turn and slay thee; and with a good heart, hereafter, should I pray to Zeus. But it is time for supper, and I would that my men were returned that we might make ready a meal."

While he spake, the swine and the swineherds drew near; and Eumaeus called to his fellows, saying: "Bring the best of the swine, for I would entertain a guest who comes from far. Verily, we endure much toil for these beasts, while others devour them, and make no return."

So they brought a hog of five years old; and the swineherd kindled a fire, and when he had cast bristles from the hog into the fire, to do honour to the gods, he slew the beast, and made ready the flesh. Seven portions he made; one he set apart for the nymphs and for Hermes, and of the rest he gave one to each. But Ulysses had the chief portion, even the chine.

Then was Ulysses glad, and spake, saying, "Eumaeus, mayest thou be dear to Zeus, for thou hast dealt kindly with me."

And Eumaeus answered: "Eat, stranger, and make merry with what thou hast. The gods give some things, and some things they withhold."

Now the night was cold, and it rained without ceasing; for the west wind, that ever bringeth rain, was blowing; and Ulysses was minded to try the swineherd, whether he would give him his own mantle, or bid another do so. Therefore, when they were about to sleep, he said:—

"Listen to me. O that I was young, and my strength unbroken, as in the days when we fought before the city of Troy.

"Once upon a time we laid an ambush near to the city of Troy. And Menelaus and Ulysses and I were the leaders of it. In the reeds we sat, and the night was cold, and the snow lay upon our shields. Now all the others had cloaks, but I had left mine behind at the ships. So, when the night was three parts spent, I spake to Ulysses, 'Here am I without a cloak; soon, methinks, shall I perish with the cold.' Soon did he bethink him of a remedy, for he was ever ready with counsel. Therefore he said: 'Hush, lest some one hear thee; and to the others, 'I have been warned in a dream. We are very far from the ships, and in peril. Therefore, let some one run to the ships, to King Agamemnon, that he send more men to help.' Then one rose up and ran, casting off his cloak; and this I took, and slept warmly therein. Were I this night such as then I was, I should not lack such kindness even now."

Then said Eumaeus: "This is well spoken, old man. Thou shalt have a cloak to cover thee. But in the morning thou must put on thy own rags again.

Yet, perchance, when the son of Ulysses shall come, he will give thee new garments."

Thereupon he arose, and set a bed for Ulysses, making it with sheepskins and goatskins, near to the fire; and when Ulysses lay down, he cast a thick cloak over him, that he had in case a great storm should arise. But he himself slept beside the boars, to guard them; and Ulysses was glad to see that he was very careful for his master's substance, even though he was so long time away.

CHAPTER XVI
THE RETURN OF TELEMACHUS

Now all this time Telemachus tarried in Sparta with King Menelaus, and the son of Nestor was with him. To him, therefore, Athene went. Nestor's son she found overcome with slumber, but Telemachus could not sleep for thoughts of his father. And Athene stood near him, and spake:—

"It is not well, Telemachus, that thou shouldest tarry longer away from thy home, for there are some who spoil and devour thy substance. Come, therefore, rouse thy host Menelaus, and pray him that he send thee on thy way. For thy mother's father and her brethren urge her to take Eurymachus [Footnote: Eu-rym'-a-chus.] for her husband, seeing that he hath far surpassed all the other suitors in his gifts. Hearken also to another matter. The bravest of the suitors lie in wait for thee in the strait that is between Ithaca and Samos, desirous to slay thee before thou shalt come again to thy home. Keep thy ship, therefore, far from the place, and sail both by night and by day, and one of the gods shall send thee a fair breeze. Also, when thou comest to the land of Ithaca, send thy ship and thy company to the city, but seek thyself the swineherd Eumaeus, for he hath been ever true to thee. Rest there the night, and bid him go to the city on the day following, and carry tidings to thy mother of thy safe return."

Then Telemachus woke the son of Nestor, touching him with his heel, and saying: "Awake, son of Nestor, bring up thy horses, and yoke them to the chariot, that we may go upon our way."

But Peisistratus made answer: "We may not drive through the darkness, how eager soever we be to depart. Soon will it be dawn. Tarry thou till Menelaus shall bring his gifts and set them on the car, and send thee on thy way, for a guest should take thought of the host that showeth him kindness."

And when the morning was come, and Menelaus was risen from his bed, Telemachus spake to him, saying, "Menelaus, send me now with all speed to my own country, for I am greatly desirous to go there."

To him Menelaus made answer: "I will not keep thee long, seeing that thou desirest to return. But stay till I bring my gifts and set them in the chariot. Let me also bid the women prepare the meal in my hall, for it is both honour to me and a profit to you that ye should eat well before ye set forth on a far journey. But if thou wilt go further through the land, then let me go with thee; to many cities will we go, and none will send us empty away."

But Telemachus said: "Not so, Menelaus; rather would I go back straightway to mine own land, for I left none to watch over my goods. It were ill done were I to perish seeking my father, or to lose some precious possession out of my house."

Then Menelaus bade his wife and the maids prepare the meal, and his squire he bade kindle a fire and roast flesh; and he himself went to his treasury, and Helen and his son with him. He himself took therefrom a double cup, and bade his son bear a mixing-bowl of silver; as for Helen, she took from her chests a robe that she had wrought with her own hands. The fairest it was of all, and shone as shines a star, and it lay beneath all the rest.

Then said Menelaus: "Take this mixing-bowl; it is wrought of silver, but the lips are finished with gold; the god Hephaestus [Footnote: He-phaes'-tus.] wrought it with his own hands, and the King of the Sidonians [Footnote: Si-do'-ni-ans.] gave it me. This cup also I give thee."

And beautiful Helen came, holding the robe in her hands, and spake, saying: "Take, dear child, this memorial of Helen's handiwork; keep it against thy marriage day, for thy bride to wear. Meanwhile, let thy mother have charge of it. And now mayest thou return with joy to thy native country and thy home!"

Then they sat down to eat and drink; and when they had finished, then did Telemachus and Nestor's son yoke the horses and climb into the chariot.

But Menelaus came forth bringing wine in a cup of gold, that they might pour out an offering to the gods before they departed. And he stood before the horses, and spake, saying:—

"Farewell, gallant youths, and salute Nestor for me; verily, he was as a father to me, when we were waging war against Troy."

To him Telemachus made answer: "That will we do; and may the gods grant that I find my father at home and tell him what grace I have found in thy sight!"

But even as he spake there flew forth at his right hand an eagle, carrying a goose in his claws, that he had snatched from the yard, and men and women followed it with loud shouting. Across the horses it flew, still going to the right; and they were glad when they saw it.

Then said Nestor's son: "Think, Menelaus! Did Zeus send this sign to us or thee?"

But while Menelaus pondered the matter, Helen spake, saying: "Hear me while I say what the gods have put in my heart. Even as this eagle came down from the hill where he was bred, and snatched away the goose from the house, so shall Ulysses come back to his home after many wanderings, and take vengeance; yea, even now he is there, plotting evil for the suitors."

Then they departed and sped across the plain. But when they came the next day to Pylos, Telemachus said to Peisistratus: "Son of Nestor, wilt thou be as a friend to me, and do my bidding? Leave me at my ship; take me not past, lest the old man, thy father, keep me out of his kindness against my will, for, indeed, I am desirous to go home."

And Nestor's son did so. He turned his horses towards the shore and the ship. And coming there, he took out the gifts, and laid them in the hinder part of the ship. This done, he called Telemachus and said: "Climb now into thy ship, and depart, ere I can reach my home. Well I know that my father will come down, and bid thee return with him to his house; nor, indeed, if he find thee here, will he go back without thee, so wilful is he of heart."

And Telemachus bade his companions climb on the ship; and they did so.

So they departed; and Athene sent a wind that blew from behind, and they sped on their way.

Meanwhile Ulysses sat with the swineherd and his men, and supped. And Ulysses, willing to try the man's temper, said: "In the morning I would fain go to the city, to the house of Ulysses, for I would not be burdensome to thee. Perchance the suitors might give me a meal. Well could I serve them. No man can light a fire, or cleave wood, or carve flesh, or pour out wine, better than I."

"Nay," said the swineherd, "thou hadst best not go among the suitors, so proud and lawless are they. They that serve them are not such as thou. They are young, and fair, and gaily clad, and their heads are anointed with oil. Abide here; thou art not burdensome to us; and when the son of Ulysses shall come, he will give thee, may be, a mantle and a tunic."

Ulysses answered: "Now may Zeus bless thee for thy kindness, for thou makest me to cease from my wanderings. Surely, nothing is more grievous to a man than to wander; but hunger compels him. Tell me now about the mother of Ulysses and about his father. Are they yet alive?"

Then said the swineherd: "I will tell thee all. Laertes, the father of Ulysses, yet lives; yet doth he daily pray to die, for he sorroweth for his son, who is far away from his home, and for his wife, who is dead. Verily, it was her death that brought him to old age before his time. And it was of grief for her son that she died. Much kindness did I receive at her hands, while she yet lived; but now I lack it. As for my lady Penelope, a great trouble hath fallen upon her house, even a plague of evil-minded men."

CHAPTER XVII
ULYSSES AND TELEMACHUS

Telemachus in his ship came safe to the island of Ithaca, at the place that was nearest to the swineherd's house. There they beached the ship, and made it fast with anchors at the fore part and hawsers at the stern, and they landed, and made ready a meal.

When they had had enough of meat and drink, Telemachus said: "Take now the ship to the city. I will come thither in the evening, having first seen my farm; and then I will pay you your wages."

Now the herdsman and Ulysses had kindled a fire, and were making ready breakfast.

And Ulysses heard the steps of a man, and, as the dogs barked not, he said to Eumaeus, "Lo! there comes some comrade or friend, for the dogs bark not."

And as he spake, Telemachus stood in the doorway; and the swineherd let fall from his hand the bowl in which he was mixing wine, and ran to him and kissed his head and his eyes and his hands. As a father kisses his only son, coming back to him from a far country after ten years, so did the swineherd kiss Telemachus. And when Telemachus came in, the false beggar, though indeed he was his father, rose, and would have given place to him; but Telemachus allowed him not to do so. And when they had eaten and drunk, Telemachus asked of the swineherd who this stranger might be.

Then the swineherd told him what he had heard, and afterwards said, "I hand him to thee; do as thou wilt."

But Telemachus answered: "Nay, Eumaeus. For am I master in my house? Do not the suitors devour it? And does not my mother doubt whether she will abide with me, remembering the great Ulysses, who was her husband, or will follow some one of those who are suitors to her? I will give this stranger, indeed, food and clothing and a sword, and will send him whithersoever he will, but I would not that he should go among the suitors, so haughty are they and violent."

Then said Ulysses: "But why dost thou bear with these men? Do the people hate thee, that thou canst not avenge thyself on them? and hast thou not kinsmen to help thee? As for me, I would rather die than see such shameful things done in a house of mine."

And Telemachus answered: "My people hate me not; but as for kinsmen, I have none, for my grandfather had but one son, Laertes, and he but one, Ulysses, and Ulysses had none other but me. Therefore do these men spoil my substance, and, it may be, will take my life also. These things, however, the gods will order. But do thou, Eumaeus, go to Penelope, and tell her that I am returned; and let no man know thereof, for they plan evil against me; but I will stay here meanwhile."

So Eumaeus departed. And when he had gone, Athene came, like a woman tall and fair; but Telemachus saw her not, for it is not given to all to see the immortal gods; but Ulysses saw her, and the dogs saw her, and whimpered for fear. She signed to Ulysses, and he went forth, and she said:—

"Hide not the matter from thy son, but plan with him how ye may slay the suitors, and lo! I am with you."

Then she touched him with her golden wand. First she put about him a fresh robe of linen and new tunic. Also she made him larger and fairer to behold. More dark did he grow, and his cheeks were rounded again, and the beard spread out black upon his chin.

Having so done, she passed away. But when Ulysses went into the hut, his son looked at him, greatly marvelling. Indeed, he feared that it might be some god.

"Stranger," he said, "surely thou art not what thou wast but a moment since; other garments hast thou, and the colour of thy skin is changed. Verily, thou must be some god from heaven. Stay awhile, that we may offer to thee sacrifice, so shalt thou have mercy on us!"

Ulysses made answer, "I am no god; I am thy father, for whom thou hast sought with much trouble of heart."

So saying, he kissed his son, and let fall a tear, but before he had kept in his tears continually.

But Telemachus, doubting yet whether this could indeed be his father, made reply: "Thou canst not be my father; some god deceiveth me that I may have sorrow upon sorrow. No mortal man could contrive this, making himself now young, now old, at his pleasure. A moment since thou wast old, and clad in vile garments; now thou art as one of the gods in heaven."

But Ulysses answered him, saying: "Telemachus, it is not fitting for thee to marvel so much at thy father's coming home. It is indeed my very self who am come, now at last in the twentieth year, having suffered many things and wandered over many lands. And this at which thou wonderest is Athene's work; she it is that maketh me now like to an old man and a beggar and now to a young man clad in rich raiment."

So speaking, he sat him down again, and Telemachus threw himself upon his father's neck and wept, and his father wept also. And when they had dried their tears, Telemachus said, "Tell me how thou camest back, my father?"

So Ulysses told him, saying: "The Phaeacians brought me back from their country while I slept. Many gifts did they send with me. These have I hidden in a cave. And to this place have I come by the counsel of Athene, that we may plan together for the slaying of the suitors. But come, tell me the number of the suitors, how many they are and what manner of men. Shall we twain be able to make war upon them or must we get the help of others?"

Then said Telemachus: "Thou art, I know, a great and wise warrior, my father, but this thing we cannot do; for these men are not ten, no, nor twice ten, but from Dulichium [Footnote: Du-lich'-i-um.] come fifty and two, and from Samos four and twenty, and from Zacynthus [Footnote: Za-cyn'-thus.] twenty, and from Ithaca twelve; and they have Medon, the herald, and a minstrel also, and attendants."

Then said Ulysses: "Go thou home in the morning and mingle with the suitors, and I will come as an old beggar; and if they treat me shamefully, endure to see it, yea, if they drag me to the door. Only, if thou wilt, speak to them prudent words; but they will not heed thee, for indeed their doom is near. Heed this also: when I give thee a sign, take all the arms from the dwelling and hide them in thy chamber. And when they shall ask thee why thou doest thus, say that thou takest them out of the smoke, for that they are not such as Ulysses left behind him when he went to Troy, but that the smoke has soiled them. Say, also, that perchance they might stir up strife sitting at their cups, and that it is not well that arms should be at hand, for that the very steel draws on a man to fight. But keep two swords and two spears and two shields—these shall be for thee and me. Only let no one know of my coming back—not Laertes, nor the swineherd; no, nor Penelope herself."

Meanwhile the ship of Telemachus came to the city, and a herald went to the palace with tidings for Penelope, lest she should be troubled for her son. So these two, the herald and the swineherd, came together, having the same errand. The herald spake out among the handmaids, saying: "O Queen, thy son is returned from Pylos!" But the swineherd went up to Penelope by herself, and told her all that Telemachus had bidden him to say. When he had so done, he turned about, and went home to his house and to the swine.

But the suitors were troubled in heart; and Eurymachus said: "This is a bold thing that Telemachus hath done. He hath accomplished his journey, which we said he never would accomplish. Let us, therefore, get rowers together, and send a ship, that we may bid our friends come back with all the speed they may."

But even while he spake, Amphinomus [Footnote: Am-phi'-no-mus.] turned him about, and saw the ship in the harbour, and the men lowering the sails. Then he laughed and said: "No need is there to send a message, for the men themselves have come. Maybe some god hath told them; maybe they saw the ship of Telemachus go by, and could not overtake it."

Then all the suitors went together to the place of assembly, and Antinous stood up and spake: "See how the gods have delivered this man! All day long our scouts sat and watched upon the headlands, one man taking another's place; and at sunset we rested not on the shore, but sailed on the sea, waiting for the morning. Yet some god hath brought him home. Nevertheless, we will bring him to an evil end, for so long as he liveth we shall not accomplish our end. Let us make haste before he assemble the people and tell them how we plotted against him. Then will they hate us, and we shall be driven forth from the land. Let us slay him, therefore, either in the field or by the way; and let us divide his possessions, but his house will we give to his mother and to him who shall marry her."

Then spake Amphinomus,—not one of the suitors was of a more understanding heart than he,—"Friends, I would not that Telemachus should be slain; it is a fearful thing to slay the son of a king. First, let us ask counsel of the gods. If the oracles of Zeus approve, then will I slay him with mine own hand; but if they forbid, then I would have you refrain."

Thereupon they departed from the place of assembly, and went to the house of Ulysses.

Now Penelope had heard from Medon, the herald, how the suitors had plotted to slay her son; therefore she went to the hall, and her maidens with her, and stood in the door, holding her veil before her face, and spake, saying:—

"Antinous, men say that thou art the best in counsel and speech of all the princes of Ithaca. But, in truth, I do find thee thus. Dost thou plot against the life of my son, having no regard for the gods, nor any memory of good deeds? Dost thou not remember how thy father fled to this house, fearing the anger of the people? Yet it is this man's house that thou dost waste, and his son that thou wouldest slay."

But Eurymachus made answer: "Take courage, wise Penelope, and let not thy heart be troubled. The man is not, nor shall be born, who shall raise a hand against Telemachus, so long as I live upon the earth. Many a time hath Ulysses set me upon his knees, and given me roasted flesh, and held the wine-cup to my lips. Therefore Telemachus is the dearest of men to me. Fear not death for him from the suitors."

So he spake, as if he would comfort her; but all the while he plotted the death of her son.

After this she went to her chamber, and wept for her lord till Athene dropped sweet sleep upon her eyes.

Meanwhile the swineherd went back to his home. But before he came Athene changed Ulysses again into the likeness of a beggar man, lest he should know him and tell the matter to Penelope.

Telemachus spake to him, saying: "What news is there in the city? Are the suitors come back from their ambush, or do they still watch for my ship?"

Eumaeus answered: "I did not think to go about the city asking questions; but I will tell what I know. The messenger from thy company joined himself to me, and, indeed, was the first to tell the news to the Queen. This also I know, that I saw a ship entering the harbour, and that there were many men in her, and spears, and shields. These, perchance, were the suitors, but I know not of a certainty."

Then Telemachus looked to his father, but the swineherd's eye he shunned.

CHAPTER XVIII
ULYSSES IN HIS HOME

When the morning came, Telemachus said to the swineherd: "I go to the city, for my mother will not be satisfied till she see my very face. And do thou lead this stranger to the city, that he may there beg his bread from any that may have the mind to give."

Thereupon Ulysses spake, saying, "I too, my friend, like not to be left here. It is better for a man to beg his bread in the town than in the fields. Go thou, and I will follow, so soon as the sun shall wax hot, for my garments are exceeding poor, and I fear lest the cold overcome me."

So Telemachus went his way, devising evil against the suitors all the while. And when he came to the house his nurse Eurycleia saw him first, and kissed him. Penelope also came down from her chamber, and cast her arms about him, and kissed him on the face, and on both the eyes, and spake, saying: "Thou art come, Telemachus, light of mine eyes! I thought not ever to see thee again. But tell me, what news didst thou get of thy father?"

And Telemachus related what Nestor and Menelaus had told him.

Meanwhile the suitors were disporting themselves, casting weights and aiming with spears in a level place. And when it was the time for supper, Medon, the herald, said, "Come now, let us sup; meat in season is a good thing."

So they made ready a feast.

Now in the meanwhile Eumaeus and the false beggar were coming to the city. And when they were now near to it, Melanthius [Footnote: Me-lan'-thi-us.], the goatherd, met them, and spake evil to Eumaeus, rebuking him because he brought this beggar to the city. And he came near and smote Ulysses with his foot on the thigh, but moved him not from the path. And Ulysses thought awhile, should he smite him with his club and slay him, or dash him on the ground. But it seemed to him better to endure.

So they went on to the palace. And at the door of the court there lay the dog Argus, whom in the old days Ulysses had reared with his own hand. But ere the dog grew to his full, Ulysses had sailed to Troy. And while he was strong, men used him in the chase, hunting wild goats and roe-deer and hares. But now he lay on a dunghill, and vermin swarmed upon him. Well he knew his master, and, although he could not come near to him, he wagged his tail and drooped his ears.

And Ulysses, when he saw him, wiped away a tear, and said, "Surely this is strange, Eumaeus, that such a dog of so fine a breed should lie here upon a dunghill."

And Eumaeus made reply: "He belongeth to a master who died far away. For, indeed, when Ulysses had him of old, he was the strongest and swiftest of dogs; but now my dear lord has perished far away, and the careless women tend him not. For when the master is away the slaves are careless of their duty. Surely a man, when he is made a slave, loses half the virtue of a man."

And as he spake the dog Argus died. Twenty years had he waited, and saw his master at the last. After this the two entered the hall. And Telemachus, when he saw them, took from the basket bread and meat, as much as his hands could hold, and bade carry them to the beggar, and also to tell him that he might go round among the suitors, asking alms. So he went, stretching out his hand, as though he were wont to beg; and some gave, having compassion upon him, and some asked who he was. But of all, Antinous was the most shameless. For when Ulysses came to him and told him how he had had much riches and power in former days, and how he had gone to Egypt, and had been sold a slave into Cyprus, Antinous mocked him, saying:—

"Get thee from my table, or thou shalt find a worse Egypt and a harder Cyprus than before."

Then Ulysses said, "Surely thy soul is evil though thy body is fair; for though thou sittest at another man's feast, yet wilt thou give me nothing."

Then Antinous caught up the footstool that was under his feet, and smote Ulysses therewith. But he stood firm as a rock; and in his heart he thought on revenge. So he went and sat down at the door. And being there, he said:—

"Hear me, suitors of the Queen! Antinous has smitten me because that I am poor. May the curse of the hungry light on him therefor, ere he come to his marriage day!"

Then spake Antinous, "Sit thou still, stranger, and eat thy bread in silence, lest the young men drag thee from the house, or strip thy flesh from off thy bones."

So he spake in his insolence; but the others blamed him, saying: "Antinous, thou didst ill to smite the wanderer; there is a doom on such deeds, if there be any god in heaven. Verily, the gods oft times put on the shape of men, and go through cities, spying out whether there is righteous dealing or unrighteous among them."

But Antinous heeded not. As for Telemachus, he nursed a great sorrow in his heart to see his father so smitten; yet he shed not a tear, but sat in silence, meditating evil against the suitors.

When Penelope also heard how the stranger had been smitten in the hall, she spake to her maidens, saying, "So may Apollo, the archer, smite Antinous!"

Then Eurynome [Footnote: Eu-ryn'-o-me.], that kept the house, made answer: "O that our prayers might be fulfilled! Surely not one of these evil men should see another day."

To her replied Penelope: "Yea, nurse, all are enemies, but Antinous is the worst. Verily, he is as hateful as death."

Then Penelope called to the swineherd and said: "Go now, and bring this stranger to me; I would greet him, and inquire of him whether he has heard tidings of Ulysses, or, it may be, seen him with his eyes, for he seems to have wandered far."

Eumaeus made answer: "Truly this man will charm thy heart, O Queen! Three days did I keep him in my dwelling, and he never ceased from telling of his sorrows. As a singer of beautiful songs charmeth men, so did he charm me. He saith that he is a Cretan, and that he hath heard of Ulysses, that he is yet alive, and that he is bringing much wealth to his home."

Then said Penelope: "Go, call the man, that I may speak with him. O that Ulysses would indeed return! Soon would he and his son avenge them of these men, for all the wrong that they have done!"

And as she spake, Telemachus sneezed, and all the house rang with the noise. And Penelope said again to Eumaeus: "Call now this stranger; didst thou not mark the good omen, how my son sneezed when I spake? Verily, this vengeance shall be wrought, nor shall one escape from it. And as for this stranger, if I shall perceive that he hath spoken truth, I will give him a new mantle and tunic."

So the swineherd spake to the stranger, saying: "Penelope would speak with thee, and would inquire concerning her husband. And if she find that thou hast spoken truth, she will give thee a mantle and a tunic, and thou shalt have freedom to beg throughout the land."

But the false beggar said: "Gladly would I tell to Penelope the story of her husband, for I know him well. But I fear these suitors. Even now, when this man struck me, and for naught, none hindered the blow, no, not Telemachus himself. Go, therefore, and bid the Queen wait till the setting of the sun."

So the swineherd went, and as he crossed the threshold Penelope said: "Thou bringest him not! What meaneth the wanderer? A beggar that is shamefaced knoweth his trade but ill."

But the swineherd answered: "He doeth well, O lady, in that he fearest the wrong-doing of these insolent men. He would have thee wait till the setting of the sun, and indeed it is better for thee to have speech with him alone."

Then said Penelope: "It is well; the stranger is a man of understanding. Verily, these men are insolent above all others."

Then the swineherd went into the throng of the suitors, and spake to Telemachus, holding his head close that none should hear: "I go to see after matters at the farm. Take thou heed of what befalleth here. Many of the people have ill-will against us. May Zeus confound them!"

Telemachus made answer, "Go, as thou sayest and come again in the morning, bringing beasts for sacrifice."

So the swineherd departed; and the suitors made merry in the hall.

CHAPTER XIX
ULYSSES IN HIS HOME

After awhile there came a beggar from the city, huge of bulk, mighty to eat and drink, but his strength was not according to his size. The young men called him Irus [Footnote: I'-rus], because he was their messenger, after Iris [Footnote: I'-ris], the messenger of Zeus. He spake to Ulysses:—

"Give place, old man, lest I drag thee forth; the young men even now would have it so, but I think it shame to strike such an one as thee."

Then said Ulysses, "There is room for thee and for me; get what thou canst, for I do not grudge thee aught, but beware lest thou anger me, lest I harm thee, old though I am."

But Irus would not hear words of peace, but still challenged him to fight.

And when Antinous saw this he was glad, and said: "This is the goodliest sport that I have seen in this house. These two beggars would fight; let us haste and match them."

And the saying pleased them; and Antinous spake again: "Hear me, ye suitors of the Queen! We have put aside these paunches of the goats for our supper. Let us agree, then, that whosoever of these two shall prevail, shall have choice of these, that which pleaseth him best, and shall hereafter eat with us, and that no one else shall sit in his place."

Then said Ulysses: "It is hard for an old man to fight with a young. Yet will I do it. Only do ye swear to me that no one shall strike me a foul blow while I fight with this man."

Then Telemachus said that this should be so, and they all consented to his words. And after this Ulysses girded himself for the fight. And all that were there saw his thighs, how great and strong they were, and his shoulders, how broad, and his arms, how mighty. And they said one to another, "There will be little of Irus left, so stalwart seems this beggar man." But as for Irus himself, he would have slunk out of sight, but they that were set to gird him compelled him to come forth.

Then said Antinous: "How is this, thou braggart, that thou fearest this old man, all woebegone as he is?"

So the two came together. And Ulysses thought whether he should strike the fellow and slay him, or fell him to the ground. And this last seemed the better of the two. So when Irus had dealt him his blow, he smote him on the jaw, and brake the bone, so that he fell howling on the ground, and the blood poured from his mouth.

Then all the suitors laughed aloud. But Ulysses dragged the fellow out of the hall, and propped him by the wall of the courtyard, putting a staff in his hand, and saying, "Sit there, and keep dogs and swine from the door, but dare not hereafter to lord it over men, no, not even ov'r strangers and beggars, lest some worse thing befall thee."

Then Antinous gave Ulysses a great paunch, and Amphinomus gave two loaves, and pledged him in a cup, saying, "Good luck to thee, hereafter, though now thou seemest to have evil fortune!"

CHAPTER XX
ULYSSES IS DISCOVERED BY HIS NURSE

And when the suitors had departed, Ulysses spake to Telemachus, saying: "Come now, let us hide away the arms that are in the hall. And if any of the suitors ask concerning them, thou shalt say, 'I have put them away out of the smoke, for they are not such as they were when Ulysses departed, for the breath of fire hath marred them. And for this cause also have I put them away, lest ye should quarrel and wound one another when ye are heated with wine; for the sight of iron tempteth a man to strike.' So shalt thou speak to the suitors."

Then said Telemachus to Eurycleia, the nurse, "Shut up the women in their chambers, till I have put away in the armoury the weapons of my father, for the smoke in the hall hath made them dim."

The nurse made answer: "I wish, my child, that thou wouldest ever have such care for thy father's possessions! But say, who shall bear the light, if thou wilt not have any of the women to go before thee?"

Then said Telemachus, "This stranger shall do it, for I will not have any man eat my bread in idleness."

So the nurse shut up the women in their chambers, and Ulysses and his son set themselves to carry the shields and the helmets and the spears, from the hall into the armoury. And Athene went ever before them, holding a lamp of gold, that shed a very fair light. Thereupon said Telemachus: "Surely, my father, this is a great wonder that I behold! See the walls, and the beams, and the pillars are bright, as it were with flames of fire. This must be the doing of a god."

But Ulysses made answer: "Hold thy peace; keep the matter in thine heart, and inquire not concerning it. And now lie down and sleep, for I would talk with thy mother."

So Telemachus went to his chamber, and slept, and Ulysses was left alone in the hall, devising in his heart how he might slay the suitors.

And now Penelope came down, and sat by the fire, on a chair cunningly wrought of silver and ivory, with a footstool that was part of the chair. And soon the maidens came in, and took away the fragments of food that were left, and the cups from which the suitors drank, and piled fresh logs on the fire.

Then Penelope called to the nurse, saying, "Nurse, bring me now a settle with a fleece upon it, that the stranger may sit and tell me his story."

So the nurse brought the settle and the fleece, and Ulysses sat him down; and Penelope spake, saying: "Stranger, I will ask thee first who art thou? Whence didst thou come? What is thy city and thy father's name?"

Ulysses made answer: "Ask me now other things as thou wilt; but ask me not of my name, or my race, or my native country, lest I weep as I think thereon, for I am a man of many sorrows; and it is not fitting to mourn and weep in the house of another."

To him Penelope made reply: "Stranger, I am sore beset with troubles. For the princes of the islands round about, yea and of Ithaca itself, woo me against my will, and devour my house. Vainly have I sought to escape their wooing. For Athene put this into my heart that I should say to them: 'Noble youths that would wed me, now that Ulysses is dead, abide patiently, though ye be eager to hasten the marriage, till I shall have finished this winding-sheet for Laertes; for it were a shame, if he, having had great wealth, should lie in his grave without a winding-sheet.' So I spake, and they gave consent. Three years did I deceive them, weaving the web by day, and by night unravelling it; but in the fourth year my handmaids betrayed me. And now I have no escape from marriage, for my parents urge me, and my son is vexed because these men devour his substance, and he is now of an age to manage his own house. But come, tell me of what race thou art; thou art not born of an oak tree or a rock, as the old fables have it."

Then said Ulysses: "If thou wilt still ask me of my race, then will I tell thee; but thou wilt so bring sorrow upon me beyond that to which I am bound; for it is grief to a man who hath wandered far and suffered much to speak of the matter."

So Ulysses told his tale. False it was, but it seemed to be true. And Penelope wept to hear it. As the snow melts upon the hills when the southeast wind bloweth, and the streams run full, so did Penelope weep for her lord. And Ulysses had compassion on his wife, when he saw her weep; but his own eyes he kept as if they had been horn or iron.

But Penelope said: "Friend, suffer me to make trial of thee, whether this was indeed my husband Ulysses. Tell me now with what raiment he was clothed, and what manner of man he was, and what his company."

Then Ulysses made answer: "I remember that he had a mantle, twofold, woollen, of sea-purple, clasped with a brooch of gold, whereon was a dog that held a fawn by the throat; marvellously wrought was the dog and the fawn. Also he had a tunic, white and smooth, even as the skin of an onion when it is dry, which the women much admired to see. But whether some one had given him these things I know not, for, indeed, many gave him gifts, and I also, even a sword and a tunic. Also he had a herald with him, one Eurybates [Footnote: Eu-ryb'-a-tes.], older than he, dark-skinned, round in the shoulders, with curly hair."

When Penelope heard this she wept yet more, for she knew by these tokens that this man was indeed her lord. "This is true," she said, "O stranger, for I myself gave him these garments, and I folded them myself, and I also gave him the jewel. And now, alas! I shall see him no more."

But Ulysses made answer: "Nay, wife of Ulysses, say not so. Cease from thy mourning, for Ulysses is yet alive. Near at hand is he, in the land of the Thesprotians, and is bringing many gifts with him. So the king of the land told me, and showed me the gifts which he had gathered; many they were and great, and will enrich his house to the tenth generation. But Ulysses himself, when I was there, had gone to Dodona [Footnote: Do-do'-na.], to inquire of Zeus—for there is the oracle of the god in the midst of an oak tree—whether he shall return to his home openly or by stealth. Be sure, O lady, that in this tenth year Ulysses shall come, even when the old moon waneth and the new is born."

Then said Penelope: "May thy words be accomplished, O stranger! Verily, thou shouldest have much kindness at my hands and many gifts. Yet I have a boding in my heart that it shall not be. But now the handmaids shall spread a bed for thee with mattress and blankets that thou mayest sleep warm till morning shall come. And they shall wash thy feet."

But Ulysses spake, saying: "Mattress and blankets have been hateful to me since I left the land of Crete. I will lie as I have been wont to lie for many nights, sleepless and waiting for the day. And I have no delight in the bath; nor shall any of these maidens touch my feet. Yet if there be some old woman, faithful of heart, her I would suffer to touch my feet."

Then said Penelope: "Such an one there is, even the woman who nursed my lord, and cherished him, and carried him in her arms, from the time when his mother bare him. She is now weak with age, but she will wash thy feet."

And she spake to the nurse, saying, "Up, now, and wash this man, who is of like age with thy master."

Then the old woman covered her face with her hands and wept, saying: "Willingly will I wash thy feet both for Penelope's sake and thine own. Many strangers, worn with travel, have come hither, but never saw I one that was so like to Ulysses in voice and in feet."

And Ulysses made answer, "Even so have I heard before; men said ever that we were most like one to the other."

But when she had made ready the bath, then Ulysses sat aloof from the hearth, and turned his face to the darkness, for he feared in his heart lest, when the old woman should handle his leg, she might know a great scar thereon, where he had been rent by the tusks of a wild boar.

By this scar, then, the old nurse knew that it was Ulysses himself, and said, "O Ulysses, O my child, to think that I knew thee not!"

And she looked towards the Queen, as meaning to tell the thing to her. But Ulysses laid his hand on her throat and said softly: "Mother, wouldest thou kill me? I am returned after twenty years, and none must know till I shall be ready to take vengeance."

And the old woman held her peace. And after this Penelope talked with him again, telling him her dreams, how she had seen a flock of geese in her palace, and how that an eagle had slain them, and when she mourned for the geese, lo! a voice that said, "These geese are thy suitors, and the eagle thy husband."

And Ulysses said that the dream was well. And then she said that on the morrow she must make her choice, for she had promised to bring forth the great bow of Ulysses, and whosoever should draw it most easily, and shoot an arrow best at a mark, he should be her husband.

And Ulysses made answer to her: "It is well, lady. Put not off this trial of the bow, for before one of them shall draw the string, the great Ulysses shall come and duly shoot at the mark that shall be set."

After this Penelope slept.

CHAPTER XXI
THE TRIAL OF THE BOW

Ulysses laid him down to sleep in the gallery of the hall. On a bull's hide he lay, and over him he put fleeces of sheep that had been slain for sacrifice and feast, and the dame that kept the house threw a mantle over him.

And he slept not, for he had many thoughts in his heart, but turned him from side to side, thinking how, being one against many, he might slay the suitors in his hall.

Then Athene came down from Olympus, and stood over his head, having taken upon herself the likeness of a woman. And she spake, saying: "Wakest thou still, man of many troubles? Is not this thy house? And is not thy wife within, and thy son, a noble lad?"

Ulysses made answer: "This is true, O goddess. But I think how I, being one against many, can slay the suitors in my hall."

Then answered the goddess: "Verily, thou art weak in faith. Some put trust in men, yet men are weaker than the gods; why trustest not thou in me? Verily, I am with thee, and will keep thee to the end. But now sleep, for to watch all the night is vexation of spirit."

So saying, she poured sleep upon his eyes and went back to Olympus.

When the morning came Ulysses awoke, and he took up the fleeces, and set them on a seat in the hall, and the bull's hide he carried without. Then he lifted up his hands to Zeus, and prayed, saying, "O Father Zeus, if thou hast led me to mine own country of good will, then give me a sign."

And even as he spake Zeus thundered from Olympus; and Ulysses heard it, and was glad. Also a woman at the mill spake a word of omen. Twelve women there were that ground the meal, wheat, and barley. Eleven of these were now sleeping, for they had finished their task; but this one, being weakest of all, was still grinding. And now she stayed her work, and said: "Surely, Father Zeus, this is a sign, for thou hast thundered in a clear sky. Grant now that this be the last meal that I shall grind for the suitors in the house of Ulysses!"

Afterwards came Telemachus, and spake to the nurse, saying, "Hast thou given to the guest food and bedding, or doth he lie uncared for?"

The nurse made answer: "The stranger drank as much as he would, and ate till he said that he had had enough; but blankets and a mattress he would not have; on an hide he slept, with fleeces of sheep above. Also we cast a mantle over him."

Next came the swineherd, leading three fatted hogs, the best of all the herd. And he said. "Stranger, do these men treat thee well?"

Ulysses made answer, "May the gods repay them as they have dealt insolently with me!"

Afterwards came Melanthius, the goatherd, having goats for the feast of the day. And he spake to Ulysses bitter words: "Wilt thou still plague us, stranger, with thy begging? Verily, I think that we shall not part till we have made trial of each other with our fists. Thy begging is not to be borne; and there are other feasts whither thou mightest go."

But Ulysses answered him not a word.

Last came Philoetius [Footnote: Phi-loe'-ti-us.], the cattleherd, bringing a heifer for the feast of the suitors. He spake to Ulysses, saying: "May happiness come to thee, stranger, hereafter! Now thou art encompassed with sorrows. Mine eyes are full of tears as I behold thee, for it may be that Ulysses is clad in vile garments like to these, wandering about among men, if, indeed, he is yet alive. But if he is dead, that, indeed, is a great sorrow. For he set me over his cattle, and these are now increased beyond all counting; never have herds increased more plentifully. Nevertheless, it vexeth my heart because strangers are ever devouring them in his hall. Verily, I would have fled long since, for the thing is past all enduring, but that I hope to see Ulysses yet come again to his own."

Then Ulysses made answer: "Cattleherd, thou art a man of an understanding heart. Now hearken to what I shall say. While thou art still in this place, Ulysses shall come home, and thou shalt see it with thine eyes, yea, and the slaying of the suitors also."

And after awhile the suitors came and sat down, as was their wont, to the feast. And the servants bare to Ulysses, as Telemachus had bidden, a full share with the others. And when Ctesippus, a prince of Samos, saw this (he was a man heedless of right and of the gods), he said: "Is it well that this fellow should fare even as we? Look now at the gift that I shall give him." Thereupon he took a bullock's foot out of a basket wherein it lay, and cast it at Ulysses.

But he moved his head to the left and shunned it, and it flew on, marking the wall. And Telemachus cried in great wrath:—

"It is well for thee, Ctesippus [Footnote: Cte-sip'-pus.], that thou didst not strike this stranger. For surely, hadst thou done this thing, my spear had pierced thee through, and thy father had made good cheer, not for thy marriage, but for thy burial."

Then said Agelaus [Footnote: A-ge-la'-us.]: "This is well said. Telemachus should not be wronged, no, nor this stranger. But, on the other hand, he must bid his mother choose out of the suitors whom she will, and marry him, nor waste our time any more."

Telemachus said: "It is well. She shall marry whom she will. But from my house I will never send against her will."

After this Penelope went to fetch the great bow of Ulysses. From the peg on which it hung she took it with its sheath, and, sitting down, she laid it on her knees and wept over it, and after this rose up and went to where the suitors sat feasting in the hall. The bow she brought, and also the quiver full of arrows, and, stalling by the pillar of the dome, spake thus:—

"Ye suitors, who devour this house, lo! here is a proof of your skill. Here is the bow of the great Ulysses. Whoever shall bend it easiest in his hands, and shoot an arrow most easily through the holes in the heads of the twelve axes that Telemachus shall set up, him will I follow, leaving this house, which I shall remember only in my dreams."

Then she bade Eumaeus bear the bow and the arrows to the suitors. And the good swineherd wept to see his master's bow, and Philoetius, the herdsman of the kine, wept also, for he was a good man, and loved the house of Ulysses.

Then Telemachus planted in order the axes wherein were the holes, and was minded himself to draw the bow; and indeed would have done the thing, but Ulysses signed to him that he should not. Therefore he said, "Methinks I am too weak and young; ye that are elder should try the first."

Then first Leiodes [Footnote: Lei-o'-des.], the priest, who alone among the suitors hated their evil ways, made trial of the bow. But he moved it not, but wearied his hands with it, for they were tender, and unaccustomed to toil. And he said, "I cannot bend this bow; let some other try; but I think that it shall be grief and pain to many this day."

And Antinous was wroth to hear such words, and bade Melanthius bring forth a roll of fat, that they might anoint the string and soften it. So they softened the string with fat, but still could they not bend it, for they all of them tried in vain, till only Antinous and Eurymachus were left, who, indeed, were the bravest and the strongest of them all.

Now the swineherd and the herdsman of the kine had gone forth out of the yard, and Ulysses came behind them and said: "What would ye do if Ulysses were to come back to his home? Would ye fight for him or for the suitors?"

And both said that they would fight for him.

And Ulysses said: "It is even I who am come back in the twentieth year, and ye, I know, are glad at heart that I am come; nor know I of any one besides. And if ye will help me as brave men to-day, wives shall ye have, and possessions and houses near to mine own. And ye shall be brothers and comrades to Telemachus. And for a sign, behold this scar which the wild boar made."

Then they wept for joy and kissed Ulysses, and he also kissed them. And he said to Eumaeus that he should bring the bow to him when the suitors had tried their fortune therewith; also that he should bid the women keep within doors, nor stir out if they should hear the noise of battle. And Philoetius he bade lock the doors of the hall, and fasten them with a rope.

After this he came back to the hall, and Eurymachus had the bow in his hands, and sought to warm it at the fire. Then he essayed to draw it, but could not. And he groaned aloud, saying: "Woe is me! not for loss of this marriage only, for there are other women to be wooed in Greece, but that we are so much weaker than the great Ulysses. This is, indeed, shame to tell."

Then said Antinous: "Not so; to-day is a holy day of the god of archers; therefore we could not draw the bow. But to-morrow will we try once more, after sacrifice to Apollo."

And this saying pleased them all; but Ulysses said, "Let me try this bow; for I would fain know whether I have such strength as I had in former days."

At this all the suitors were wroth, and chiefly Antinous, but Penelope said that it should be so, and promised the man great gifts if he could draw this bow.

But Telemachus spake thus: "Mother, the bow is mine to give or to refuse. And no man shall say me nay, if I will that this stranger make trial of it. But do thou go to thy chamber with thy maidens, and let men take thought for these things."

And this he said because he would have her depart from the hall forthwith, knowing what should happen therein. But she marvelled to hear him speak with such authority, and answered not, but departed. And when Eumaeus would have carried the bow to Ulysses, the suitors spake roughly to him, but Telemachus constrained him to go. Therefore he took the bow and gave it to his master. Then went he to Eurycleia, and bade her shut the door of the women's chambers and keep them within, whatsoever they might hear.

Then Ulysses handled the great bow, trying it, whether it had taken any hurt, but the suitors thought scorn of him. Then, when he had found it to be without flaw, just as a minstrel fastens a string upon his harp and strains it to the pitch, so he strung the bow without toil; and holding the string in his right hand, he tried its tone, and the tone was sweet as the voice of a swallow. Then he took an arrow from the quiver, and laid the notch upon the string and drew it, sitting as he was, and the arrow passed through every ring, and stood in the wall beyond. Then he said to Telemachus:—

"There is yet a feast to be held before the sun go down."

And he nodded the sign to Telemachus. And forthwith the young man stood by him, armed with spear and helmet and shield.

CHAPTER XXII
THE SLAYING OF THE SUITORS

Then spake Ulysses among the suitors: "This labour has been accomplished. Let me try at yet another mark."

And he aimed his arrow at Antinous. But the man was just raising a cup to his lips, thinking not of death, for who had thought that any man, though mightiest of mortals, would venture on such a deed, being one among many? Right through the neck passed the arrow-head, and the blood gushed from his nostrils, and he dropped the cup and spurned the table from him.

And all the suitors, when they saw him fall, leapt from their seats; but when they looked, there was neither spear nor shield upon the wall. And they knew not whether it was by chance or of set purpose that the stranger had smitten him. But Ulysses then declared who he was, saying:—

"Dogs, ye thought that I should never come back! Therefore have ye devoured my house, and made suit to my wife while I yet lived, and feared not the gods nor regarded men. Therefore a sudden destruction is come upon you all."

Then when all the others trembled for fear, Eurymachus said: "If thou be indeed Ulysses of Ithaca, thou hast said well. Foul wrong has been done to thee in the house and in the field. But lo! he who was the mover of it all lieth here, even Antinous. Nor was it so much this marriage that he sought, as to be king of this land, having destroyed thy house. But we will pay thee back for all that we have devoured, even twenty times as much."

But Ulysses said: "Speak not of paying back. My hands shall not cease from slaying till I have taken vengeance on you all."

Then said Eurymachus to his comrades: "This man will not stay his hands. He will smite us all with his arrows where he stands. But let us win the door, and raise a cry in the city; soon then will this archer have shot his last."

And he rushed on, with his two-edged knife in his hand. But as he rushed, Ulysses smote him on the breast with an arrow, and he fell forwards. And when Amphinomus came on, Telemachus slew him with his spear, but drew not the spear from the body, lest some one should smite him unawares.

Then he ran to his father and said, "Shall I fetch arms for us and our helpers?"

"Yea," said he, "and tarry not, lest my arrows be spent."

So he fetched from the armoury four shields and four helmets and eight spear. And he and the servants, Eumaeus and Philoetius, armed themselves. Also Ulysses, when his arrows were spent, donned helmet and shield, and took a mighty spear in each hand. But Melanthius, the goatherd, crept up to the armoury and brought down there from twelve helmets and shields, and spears as many. And when Ulysses saw that the suitors were arming themselves, he feared greatly, and said to his son:—

"There is treachery here. It is one of the women, or, it may be, Melanthius, the goatherd."

And Telemachus said, "This fault is mine, my father, for I left the door of the chamber unfastened."

And soon Eumaeus spied Melanthius stealing up to the chamber again, and followed him, and Philoetius with him. There they caught him, even as he took a helmet in one hand and a shield in the other, and bound his feet and hands, and fastened him aloft by a rope to the beams of the ceiling.

Then these two went back to the hall, and there also came Athene, having the shape of Mentor. Still, for she would yet further try the courage of Ulysses and his son, she helped them not as yet, but, changing her shape, sat on the roof-beam like unto a swallow.

And then cried Agelaus: "Friends, Mentor is gone, and helps them not. Let us not cast our spears at random, but let six come on together; perchance we may prevail against them."

Then they cast their spears, but Athene turned them aside, one to the pillar, and another to the door, and another to the wall. But Ulysses and Telemachus and the two herdsmen slew each his man; and yet again they did so, and again. Only Amphimedon [Footnote: Am- phim'-e-don.]wounded Telemachus, and Ctesippus grazed the shoulder of Eumaeus. But Telemachus struck down Amphimedon, and the herdsman of the kine slew Ctesippus, saying: "Take this, for the ox-foot which thou gavest to our guest." And all the while Athene waved her flaming shield from above and the suitors fell as birds are scattered and torn by eagles.

Then Leiodes, the priest, made supplication to Ulysses, saying: "I never wrought evil in this house, and would have kept others from it, but they would not. Naught have I done save serve at the altar; wherefore, slay me not."

And Ulysses made reply, "That thou hast served at the altar of these men is enough, and also that thou wouldest wed my wife."

So he slew him; but Phemius, the minstrel, he spared, for he had sung among the suitors in the hall because he had been compelled, and not of his own will; and also Medon, the herald, bidding them go into the yard without. There they sat, holding by the altar and looking fearfully every way, for they still feared that they should die.

So the slaughtering of the suitors was ended; and now Ulysses bade cleanse the hall and wash the benches and the tables with water, and purify them with sulphur; and when this was done, that Eurycleia, the nurse, should go to Penelope and tell her that her husband was indeed returned.

CHAPTER XXIII
THE END OF THE WANDERING

Eurycleia went to the chamber of her mistress, bearing the glad tidings. She made haste in her great joy, and her feet stumbled one over the other. And she stood by the head of Penelope, and spake, saying: "Awake, dear child, and see with thine eyes that which thou hast desired so long. For, indeed, Ulysses hath come back, and hath slain the men that devoured his substance."

But Penelope made answer: "Surely, dear nurse, the gods have bereft thee of thy sense; and verily, they can make the wisdom of the wise to be foolishness, and they can give wisdom to the simple. Why dost thou mock me, rousing me out of my sleep, the sweetest that hath ever come to my eyes since the day when Ulysses sailed for Troy, most hateful of cities? Go, get thee to the chamber of the women! Had another of the maids roused me in this fashion, I had sent her back with a sharp rebuke, But thine old age protects thee."

Then said the nurse: "I mock thee not, dear child. In very truth Ulysses is here. He is the stranger to whom such dishonour was done. But Telemachus knew long since who he was, and hid the matter, that they might take vengeance on the suitors."

Then was Penelope glad, and she leapt from bed, and fell upon the neck of the old woman, weeping, and saying, "Tell me now the truth, whether, indeed, he hath come home, and hath slain the suitors, he being but one man, and they many."

The nurse made answer: "How it was done I know not; only I heard the groaning of men that were slain. Amazed did we women sit in our chamber till thy son called me. Then I found Ulysses standing among the dead, who lay one upon another. Verily, thou hadst been glad at heart to see him, so like to a lion was he, all stained with blood and the labour of the fight. And now the suitors lie in a heap, and he is purifying his house with brimstone. But come, that ye may have an end of all the sorrow that ye have endured, for thy desire is fulfilled. Thy husband hath come back, and hath avenged him to the full on these evil men."

But Penelope said: "Dear nurse, be not too bold in thy joy. Thou knowest how gladly I would see him. But this is not he; it is one of the gods that hath slain the suitors, being wroth at their insolence and wrong-doing. But Ulysses himself hath perished."

Then the nurse spake, saying: "What is that thou sayest? That thy husband will return no more, when he is even now in his own house? Nay, thou art, indeed, slow to believe. Hear now this manifest token that I espied with mine eyes,—the scar of the wound that long since a wild boar dealt him with his tusk. I saw it when I washed his feet, and would fain have told thee, but he laid his hand upon my mouth, and in his wisdom suffered me not to speak."

To her Penelope made answer: "It is hard for thee to know the purposes of the gods. Nevertheless, I will go to my son, that I may see the suitors dead, and the man that slew them."

So she went and sat in the twilight by the other wall, and Ulysses sat by a pillar, with eyes cast down, waiting till his wife should speak to him. But she was sore perplexed; for now she seemed to know him, and now she knew him not, for he had not suffered that the women should put new robes upon him.

And Telemachus said: "Mother, evil mother, sittest thou apart from my father, and speakest not to him? Surely thy heart is harder than a stone."

But Ulysses said: "Let be, Telemachus. Thy mother will know that which is true in good time. But now let us hide this slaughter for awhile, lest the friends of these men seek vengeance against us. Wherefore, let there be music and dancing in the hall, so that men shall say, 'This is the wedding of the Queen, and there is joy in the palace,' and know not of the truth."

So the minstrel played and the women danced. And meanwhile Ulysses went to the bath, and clothed himself in bright apparel, and came back to the hall, and Athene made him fair and young to see. Then he sat him down as before, over against his wife, and said:—

"Surely, O lady, the gods have made thee harder of heart than all other women. Would another wife have kept away from her husband, coming back now after twenty years?"

And when she doubted yet, he spake again: "Hear thou this, Penelope, and know that it is I indeed. I will tell thee of the fashion of my bed. There grew an olive in the inner court, with a stem of the bigness of a pillar. Round this did I build the chamber, and I roofed it over, and put doors upon it. Then I lopped off the boughs of the olive, and made it into the bedpost. Afterwards, beginning from this, I wrought the bedstead till I had finished it, inlaying the work with gold and silver and ivory. And within I fastened a band of ox-hide that had been dyed with purple. Whether the bedstead be now fast in its place, or whether some one hath moved it—and verily, it was no light thing to move —I know not. But this was its fashion of old."

Then Penelope knew him, that he was her husband indeed, and ran to him, and threw her arms about him and kissed him, saying: "Pardon me, my lord, if I was slow to know thee; for ever I feared that some one should deceive me, saying that he was my husband. But now I know this, that thou art he and not another."

And they wept over each other and kissed each other. So did Ulysses come back to his home after twenty years.

CHAPTER XXIV
THE TRIUMPH OF ULYSSES

Meanwhile, Ulysses went forth from his palace to the dwelling of Laertes, that was in the fields. There the old man dwelt, and a woman of Sicily cared for him. And Ulysses spake to his son and to the shepherds, saying: "Go ye into the house and prepare a meal of swine's flesh, as savoury as may be; and I will make trial of my father, whether he will know me. For it may well be that he hath forgotten me, seeing that I have been now a long time absent."

So spake Ulysses, and gave also his arms to the men to keep for him. So they went into the house. And Ulysses went to the orchard, making search for his father. There he found not Dolius [Footnote: Do'-li-us.], that was steward to Laertes, nor any one of his servants, nor of his sons, for they were gone to make a fence about the field. Only the old man he found; and he was busy digging about a tree. Filthy was the tunic that he had about him and sewn with thread; and he had coverings of ox-hide on his legs to keep them from the thorns, and gloves upon his hands, and a cap of dog-skin on his head. And when Ulysses saw him, how that he was worn with old age and very sorrowful, he stood under a pear tree and wept. Then for awhile he took counsel with himself, whether he should kiss his father and embrace him, and make himself known, and tell him how he had come back to his home, or should first inquire of him, and learn all that he would know. And he judged it best first to inquire. So he came near to the old man; and the old man was digging about a tree, having his head bent down.

Then said Ulysses: "Verily, old man, thou lackest not skill to deal with an orchard. And truly, neither fig, nor vine, nor olive, nor pear may flourish in a garden without care. But yet another thing will I say to thee, and be not thou wroth when thou hearest it. Thy garden, indeed, is well cared for, but thou thyself art in evil plight. For old age lieth heavy upon thee, and thou art clad in filthy garments. Yet truly it is not because thou art idle that thy master thus dealeth with thee; nor, indeed, art thou in any wise like unto a slave; for thy face and thy stature are as it might be of a king. Such an one as thou art should wash himself, and sit down to meat, and sleep softly; for such is the right of old age. But come, tell me truly, whose servant art thou? Whose orchard dost thou tend? Tell me this also: is this, indeed, the land of Ithaca to which I am come? This, indeed, a certain man that I met as I came hither told me, but he seemed to be but of simple mind, nor would he listen to my words, nor tell me of a friend that I have who dwelleth in this place, whether he be alive or dead. I entertained him a long time since in my house, and never was there stranger whom I loved more than him. And he said that he was the son of Laertes, and that he came from the land of Ithaca."

To him Laertes made answer, weeping the while: "Doubt not, stranger, that thou art come to the land of which thou inquirest. But unrighteous and violent men have it in possession. But as for the son of Laertes, hadst thou found him here, verily, he would have sent thee away with many gifts. But tell me truly, is it long time since thou didst give him entertainment? For, indeed, he is my son, unhappy man that I am. Surely either he hath been drowned in the sea, and the fishes have devoured him, or wild beasts and birds of the air have eaten him upon the land. And neither father nor mother, nor his wife, Penelope, most prudent of women, could make lamentation for him and lay him out for his burial. But tell me, who art thou? Where is thy city, and what thy parentage? Did thine own ship bring thee hither, and thy companions with thee, or didst thou come as a trader upon the ship of another?"

Then said Ulysses: "All this I will tell thee truly. My name is Eperitus.[Footnote: E-per'-i-tus.] It was of the doing of the gods that I came hither from the land of Sicily, and not of mine own will. And my ship is moored hard by. As for Ulysses, it is now the fifth year since he left me. Yet verily, the omens were good when he went forth on his journey, so that we both rejoiced, thinking that he would journey safely, and that we should be friends the one to the other in the time to come."

So spake Ulysses; and when the old man, his father, heard these words, great grief came upon him, and he took up the dust in his hands and poured it upon the white hairs of his head. And the heart of Ulysses was moved within him as he saw it, and he was ready to weep when he beheld his father. Then he threw his arms about him and kissed him, and said: "My father, here am I, thy son for whom thou weepest. Lo! I am come back to my native country after twenty years, and I have avenged myself on them that sought my wife in marriage, slaying them all."

To him the old man made answer, "If thou art my very son Ulysses, tell me some clear sign whereby I may know thee."

Then said Ulysses: "See, now, this scar upon my thigh where the wild boar wounded me on Mount Parnassus.[Footnote: Par nas'-sus.] For thou and my mother sent me to my grandfather, and I was wounded in the hunting. And let this also be a sign to thee. I will tell thee what trees of the orchard thou gavest me long since, when I was a boy and walked with thee, inquiring of thee their names. Thirteen pear trees didst thou give me, and ten apple trees, and of fig trees two score. Fifty rows also of vines didst thou promise to give me when the time of grapes should come."

And the old man's heart was moved within him, and his knees failed him, for he knew that the signs were true. And he threw his arms about his son, and the spirit of the old man revived, and he said: "Now I know that there are gods in heaven when I hear that these evil men have been punished for their wrong-doing. Nevertheless, I fear much lest their kinsmen shall stir up the men of Ithaca and of the islands round about against us."

Then said Ulysses: "Trouble not thyself with these matters, my father. Let us go rather to the house. There are Telemachus and Eumaeus, and the keeper of the herds, and they have made ready, that we may dine."

So they went to the house, and found Telemachus and his companions cutting flesh for the dinner and mixing the wine. Then the woman of Sicily washed the old man Laertes and anointed him with oil, and clad him in a fair cloak. And Athene also stood by him, and made him taller and sturdier to look on than before. And his son marvelled to behold him, so fair he was and like to the gods that live forever, so that he spake to him, saying, "O my father, surely one of the gods that live forever hath made thee fair to look upon and tall!"

And Laertes made answer: "Would to God that I had stood by you yesterday, taking vengeance on the suitors, with the strength I had of old. Many a man would I have slain with my spear, and thou wouldest have rejoiced in thy heart."

Thus spake they together. And when the dinner was ready they sat down to meat; and the old man Dolius, with his sons, approached, coming in from their labour; for the woman of Sicily, that was the mother of the lads, had called them. And when they saw Ulysses, they stood amazed and speechless. And Ulysses said, "Cease to wonder, old man, at this sight, and sit down to meat; truly we are ready for our meat, and have waited long time for you."

Then Dolius ran to him, stretching forth both his hands, and caught the hand of Ulysses and kissed it on the wrist. And he spake, saying: "Right glad are we at thy coming, for we looked not for thee. Surely it is of the gods that thou hast returned. May all things be well with thee. But tell me this. Knoweth Queen Penelope of thy coming, or shall I send a messenger to tell her?"

"Verily, she knoweth it," said Ulysses. Then the old man sat down to meat, and his sons also, when they had greeted Ulysses.

In the meanwhile there spread through the city the tidings how the suitors had been slain; and the kindred of the men came to the house of Ulysses with many groans and tears, and carried away the dead bodies and buried them. But such as came from other lands they put on shipboard, that they might carry them to the sepulchres of their fathers. And when these things were ended they gathered themselves together in the marketplace; and Eupeithes [Footnote: Eu-pei'-thes.] stood up amongst them, being sore troubled in his heart for his son Antinous, whom Ulysses had slain first of all the suitors. He stood up, therefore, in the midst, and spake: "Surely this man hath wrought great evils in this land. First he took comrades with him to Troy, many in number and brave. These all he lost, and their ships also. And now he hath come hither and slain the princes of the people. Shame it were to us, yea, among the generations to come, if we avenge not ourselves on them that have slain our sons and our brothers. Verily, I desire not life, if such should go unpunished. Come, therefore, let us make haste, lest they cross over the sea and so escape."

So Eupeithes spake, weeping the while. And all the people had pity to hear him. But Medon, the herald, stood up in the assembly and spake, saying: "Hear me, men of Ithaca! Verily, Ulysses did not all these things without the helping of the gods that live forever. I, indeed, saw with mine own eyes one of the gods standing by Ulysses, being like to Prince Mentor in shape. By Ulysses there stood a god, and strengthened him; and another was there among the suitors, troubling them so that they fell."

Thus spake Medon, the herald, and after him stood up Alitherses [Footnote: A-li-ther'-ses.], the seer, that knew all things that had been and should be hereafter, and spake, saying: "It is of your folly, ye men of Ithaca, that all these things have come to pass. Ye would not hearken to me, no, nor to Mentor, nor would ye restrain your sons from their folly. Great wickedness did they work, wasting the goods of a brave man, and making suit to his wife, for they thought not that he would return. Come now, hearken unto me, lest some worse evil befall you."

Then some indeed rose up and made haste to depart; and these were the greater part; but the others remained in their places, for they liked not the counsel of Medon and the seer, but regarded the words of Eupeithes. Then they clad themselves in their armour and marched to the city, Eupeithes leading them.

Then spake Athene to Zeus: "Tell me, my father, what dost thou purpose in thy heart? Wilt thou that there be strife or friendship between these two?"

To her Zeus made answer: "Why dost thou inquire this thing of me? Was it not of thy contriving that Ulysses slew the suitors in his palace? Order it as thou wilt. But let there be peace and friendship in the end, that Ulysses may prosper in the land, and the people dwell in happiness about him."

Then Athene departed, and came to the land of Ithaca.

And when Ulysses and they that sat with him had made an end of eating and drinking, the King said, "Let some one go forth and see whether these men are near at hand."

So the son of Dolius went forth. And as he stood on the threshold he saw them approaching, and cried: "They are even now close at hand; let us arm ourselves in all haste."

So they armed themselves. With Ulysses were Telemachus, and Eumaeus, and the keeper of the herds. Also there stood with him six sons of Dolius; and the two old men also, Laertes and Dolius, though their heads were white with age. And as they went forth from the house Athene came near, having the form and the voice of Prince Mentor. And when Ulysses saw her, he was glad at heart, and spake to Telemachus, saying, "I know thee well, my son, that thou wilt bear thyself bravely, and do no dishonour to the house of thy fathers, that have ever been famous in the land for courage and manhood."

Telemachus answered, "This, my father, thou shalt see for thyself, if thou wilt."

And Laertes was glad at heart, and said, "How happy is this day, in the which my son and my grandson contend one with the other in valour."

Then Athene came near to the old man, and said, "Laertes, pray thou first to Athene and Father Zeus, and then cast thy spear."

So she spake, and breathed great strength into his heart. And having prayed, he cast his spear, and smote Eupeithes through the helmet, so that he fell dead upon the ground. Then Ulysses and his son fell upon the men of Ithaca with swords and two-handed spears. Verily, they had slain them all, but that Athene cried aloud, saying: "Cease, men of Ithaca, from the battle, for it is too hard for you."

And the men were sore afraid when they heard her voice, and threw their arms upon the ground and fled, if haply they might escape to the city. And when Ulysses would have pursued after them, Zeus cast a thunderbolt from heaven, so that it fell before the feet of Athene. And Athene cried, "Cease from the battle, son of Laertes, lest Zeus be wroth with thee."

So Ulysses was stayed from the battle; and Zeus and Athene made peace between the King and the men of Ithaca.

Milton Keynes UK
Ingram Content Group UK Ltd.
UKHW030846141124
451205UK00005B/448